D0484763

Playing
Cupid

CALGARY PUBLIC LIBRARY

JUL   2017

Playing
Cupid

Jenny Meyerhoff

SCHOLASTIC INC.

If you purchased this book without a cover, you should be aware that this book is stolen property. It was reported as "unsold and destroyed" to the publisher, and neither the author nor the publisher has received any payment for this "stripped book."

Copyright © 2016 by Jenny Meyerhoff

All rights reserved. Published by Scholastic Inc., *Publishers since 1920.* SCHOLASTIC and associated logos are trademarks and/or registered trademarks of Scholastic Inc.

The publisher does not have any control over and does not assume any responsibility for author or third-party websites or their content.

No part of this publication may be reproduced, stored in a retrieval system, or transmitted in any form or by any means, electronic, mechanical, photocopying, recording, or otherwise, without written permission of the publisher. For information regarding permission, write to Scholastic Inc., Attention: Permissions Department, 557 Broadway, New York, NY 10012.

This book is a work of fiction. Names, characters, places, and incidents are either the product of the author's imagination or are used fictitiously, and any resemblance to actual persons, living or dead, business establishments, events, or locales is entirely coincidental.

ISBN 978-1-338-09922-5

10 9 8 7 6 5 4 3 2 1   17 18 19 20 21

Printed in the U.S.A.   40
First printing 2017

Book design by Jennifer Rinaldi and Yaffa Jaskoll

For Emma

Chapter One

Emily's mom dropped us off at the side entrance of the mall. A little shiver went through me as I stepped out of the car. If they noticed, Emily and her mom would probably think the shiver was from the cold winter weather, but it was really a shiver of excitement. Not because I was at the mall. Malls aren't *that* great. The shiver was because I was actually hanging out with a friend.

"I'll be back for you at five o'clock," Emily's mom reminded us.

"Thanks, Mrs. Schmidt," I called out.

"You're welcome, Clara," she answered cheerfully.

"Thanks, Mom." Emily slid the door of the minivan shut.

She waved to her mother through the front window, then we ran inside to get out of the snow.

"What should we do first?" I asked, stamping my slushy shoes on the slatted floor of the entryway. "Freezies? Up the down escalator? Or the toy store?"

Emily pushed the button for the sliding door, and our footsteps clicked against the shiny, slick tile floor as we entered the mall. "Let's do that thing in the food court again. Remember? When you match up the couples?" Emily nodded her head enthusiastically and opened her eyes wide. "You're, like, psychic or something!"

I shrugged. It wasn't that big of a deal. I was just good at people watching, and I noticed things that others didn't. That was what happened when you were used to spending most of your time alone.

"Freezies it is!" I said.

Emily and I made our way to the food court as quickly as possible. Of course, first we stopped in the department store and pretended to be mannequins, then we rode the glass elevator up to the third floor, pointing and acting shocked at some imaginary thing in the distance (we got twelve people to look), and finally we ordered two blue raspberry Freezies and settled in at a corner booth.

"Okay," I said, scanning the food court, "that guy, over by the big plant." I pointed to a teenager wearing earbuds, a knit cap, and a T-shirt that said *Haters Gonna Hate*. I pointed with my pinkie finger so it wouldn't be too obvious.

"I see him," Emily whispered, nodding.

I put my cup in front of my mouth to block my lips while I spoke. "He doesn't have a girlfriend."

"How can you tell?" Emily asked. "Maybe she's on vacation for winter break or something."

"No way." I shook my head. "He's checking out all the girls his age who walk by. But in a shy, hopeful way. Not like he's a player. He's looking for love."

Emily sighed like that was the most romantic thing she'd ever heard. I sighed too because I knew where looking for love was going to get him. Heartbreak. I'd seen it happen with my parents and a zillion other people. Somehow, though, most everyone seemed to think love and crushes and flirting and all that stuff were still worth it. I figured if they wanted to set themselves up for pain, who was I to stop them?

"She's the one," I said, nodding my head toward a girl with curly black hair wearing a peasant skirt and big woolly boots.

Emily smiled, then took a long sip of Freezy. "I can see it," she said. "Now what?"

I pressed my fingertips together and thought. "Okay," I said. "Got it. Let's go."

Emily and I walked over to the girl first. I wasn't usually too shy about talking to strangers. I actually loved talking to all kinds of people, and that made being the one girl at my old school that nobody wanted to talk to just about the worst thing that could ever happen to me.

"Excuse me," I said. The girl had been sketching, and she flipped back the long curtain of curls that had been covering her face to look up at me. "My friend and I are doing a project for school. Extra credit," I added when she squinted her eyes suspiciously. "Over winter break."

The corners of her eyes relaxed, so I continued. "We are trying to see how many things random strangers have in common. We just need to ask you three questions."

She put her pen down and said, "Okay, I'm game."

I looked at Emily and smiled. She beamed back at me.

"Great," I said. "Would you mind stepping over to another table?" I headed toward where Headphone Guy was sitting, and Emily and the curly girl followed me. When the guy noticed me standing there, he pulled out an earbud. I explained about our fake school project and introduced Curly Girl, and he couldn't agree to participate fast enough. He pulled out the chair next to him for her to sit down.

"Cats or dogs?" I asked them.

"Dogs," they both said at the same time, then they looked at each other and laughed. I turned to Emily and raised an eyebrow. She smiled and nodded.

"What kind of music do you listen to?" Emily asked next.

Curly Girl wrapped one of her curls around a finger. "I like a lot of different music," she said. "Mostly old stuff— Joni Mitchell, Bob Marley, Dylan."

"Hey!" The guy started laughing. He held the dangling earbud up to curly girl's ear. She smiled and began bobbing her head. "I'm listening to 'Three Little Birds' right now," he told us. "That's Bob Marley."

I smiled, turned to Emily, and wagged my eyebrows. It was time for the clincher.

"What's your favorite movie?"

"*The Matrix*," the guy said. "Definitely."

"What?" Curly Girl looked at him, shocked. "I mean, *The Matrix* was good, but what about *Blade Runner*?"

A movie argument? I mentally patted myself on the back: They were practically a couple already. I turned to Emily and whispered, "I think our work here is done."

The guy grinned at Curly Girl sheepishly. "I've never seen *Blade Runner*."

The girl grabbed his arm and said, "You. Have. To. See. *Blade. Runner*."

I leaned forward over their table to get their attention. "Well, that's it. Thanks for your help, you guys."

Emily and I raced back to our table and sunk down in our seats to watch the love story unfold. Just as I expected, Curly Girl didn't go back to her spot.

"You are amazing," Emily said to me. "Look at how she keeps touching his arm as she talks."

"Ooh! They're exchanging phone numbers!" I high-fived

Emily as the guy and girl both got out their phones and began tapping away.

Fixing up random strangers in the mall didn't always work. One time, the two people actually got into a food fight, but today my instincts were sharp.

"Who's next?" Emily asked, bouncing up and down in her seat. "Can I try to pick someone?"

"Sure," I said, my eyes sliding over the food court anyway. "Wait. Isn't that Alivia?" I pointed to a tall girl with long, pin-straight black hair standing over by the frozen yogurt stand. She was waiting for an even taller girl who resembled her.

"Where?" Emily squinted as she looked back and forth. "Oh yeah," she said. "It is! She's with her sister."

Alivia and Emily were both part of the same friend group. They'd been friends since preschool.

"Should we say hi, or ask her if she wants to hang with us?" I asked. I'd been eating lunch with them for a few months now, but I was still more Emily's friend than Alivia's. I wanted to become closer friends with the whole group, though, and Alivia was their leader.

"Sure, if you want," Emily said.

"Alivia!" I waved across the food court and shouted her name again. "Alivia!"

That time she saw us. She said something to her sister, then headed over to us.

"I'm so glad you're here, you guys," Alivia said, sitting down at our table and taking a sip of Emily's Freezy. "My mom made me come to the mall with Miss Perfect. She, like, needs the world to believe the Hawkins sisters are best friends or something."

"You don't like your sister?" I asked. I used to fantasize that my babysitters were really my older sisters. I was an only child with a dad who worked all the time, so having a sibling sounded pretty good to me. The closest I had was a next-door neighbor who came over a lot.

"She's the worst!" Alivia said. "Like anything you ever want to wear, she already owns it and it looks amazing on her, and any activity you want to do, she's already done it, perfectly."

"That would be annoying," I agreed, taking a sip of my Freezy.

"So, what are you guys doing?" Alivia asked.

"We were playing Cupid," I said.

Alivia's eyes sparkled. "For who? Are Logan and Mateo and all those guys here?" Now it was her turn to search the food court. She turned back to me and lowered her voice. "I have a feeling one of them is going to ask me out when we get back to school."

"Who?" I asked, leaning forward. Alivia was actually sharing a secret with me. That was a good sign.

Alivia bit her bottom lip. "I can't tell you. I don't want to jinx it."

"Clara is really good at fixing people up," Emily told Alivia. "She can pick two random strangers and make them a couple in, like, five seconds."

"Cool. So, the guys aren't here?" Alivia asked. Emily shook her head, and Alivia huffed a breath. "Maybe they're by the sports store. Let's go shop."

"But I think you'd really like playing Cupid," Emily told her. "It's so fun."

"That's okay," I said. "I'm good with shopping."

"Great," Alivia said.

"Oh. Okay. I just have to go to the bathroom." Emily stood up. "I'll be right back," she said. Alivia took Emily's drink and pulled it to her side of the table as Emily walked off.

She leaned forward. "I'm not trying to say anything mean," Alivia told me in a low voice, "but lately, I feel like Emily doesn't seem to fit in with the rest of my friends, you know?"

I swallowed. I *didn't* know. "Really?" I asked.

"I mean, we used to be best friends, but lately it seems like we don't have anything in common." Alivia tossed some of her hair back over her shoulder. "We just, like, have different standards."

I ran my hand over my wavy dark hair, hoping it met Alivia's standards.

"Don't tell anyone, but I'm not sure I see us staying friends forever." She raised her eyebrows and pointed her chin to where Emily was walking back toward us. "We're just so different. See what I mean?"

I studied Emily, trying to figure it out. She wore stretchy black leggings and a zipper hoodie. It was practically the same outfit Alivia was wearing, except Alivia was tall and thin and Emily was short and round, so it looked sort of different. But they both looked great to me.

"I'm back," Emily said when she reached our table. "Are you guys ready?"

"Totally." Alivia stood up. "We should look for outfits for my party next weekend. My mom said I could invite the guys' group."

"I'll probably just wear what I always wear," Emily said, "but I'm happy to help you look."

Emily bounded off ahead of us, and Alivia bumped shoulders with me. "You'll look for outfits with me, right?"

I pinched myself to make sure I wasn't dreaming. Nope, I was really and truly shopping with friends. "Absolutely," I said. "I love getting dressed up."

Chapter Two

The logs in the fire crackled, and I shifted so that I could lean against the arm of the couch. Normally I loved watching the fireplace with Papi on a cold wintery Sunday afternoon, but today it wasn't so fun. Papi held my report card in both hands. It had arrived in the mail two weeks ago, but I guessed we still weren't finished discussing it.

"*Mija*, I don't understand. I know you can do better than this." My father rubbed his hand against his forehead.

"I know, Papi, I'll do better this semester, I promise."

"It's important to do well in school." He started his familiar refrain, and I shifted in my seat again. I knew his lecture by heart I'd heard it so many times. "If you don't get good grades, you won't go to college. I know you are only in seventh grade, but it's not too young to work hard."

"I know, Papi, I will."

"Your mother didn't go to college after high school," he told me for the millionth time. "If she had gone to college before we got married, maybe she could have been happy. She could have known what she wanted to do. Education is the most important thing."

I never knew what to say to my father when he started on this speech. It's not that I didn't agree with him. I knew good grades were important, but if my mother had gone to college first, I never would have been born, and sometimes it seemed like my father thought that might be a good thing.

"Papi, trust me, *por favor*. I'll do better, okay?"

I shifted again and glanced out the window. Joey, our next-door neighbor, was climbing out of the back of a green minivan. He wore a puffy black coat, a black ski cap, and thick black gloves. Before I could stop and think about what I was doing, I jumped up and ran to the door. "I'll be right back," I called to Papi, opening the door and stepping out into the freezing cold.

I slid across the front porch in the new green ballet flats I'd bought with Alivia. I should have put on my boots. My toes were probably going to go numb. I went carefully down the stairs and skated across my front walkway to meet Joey in the middle of the driveway we shared.

"Hey, stranger," I said. I hadn't seen him for all of winter break. His family had driven down to Florida. "You're back."

"Hey," Joey said, looking at my shoes. "I'm not sure if you noticed," he said, "but it's winter outside."

"Ha-ha." I wrapped my arms tightly around my body to control my shivers. "It's not *that* cold."

Joey laughed. "Right," he said, drawing the word out slowly. "It's not cold at all." He reached down, grabbed a big handful of snow, and patted it into a snowball. "You look like you feel warm and toasty. You and all your new friends are so cool, I bet winter feels like a heat wave."

"Don't be that way. They're nice. You just have to get to know them." I reached down and grabbed my own handful of snow, to prove he was wrong about the cold. And everything else. Instantly my fingers started to sting.

"No thanks," he said. "I have no interest in getting to know them."

"They can't help it if other people are jealous of them."

Joey raised his eyebrows at me, and it made his glasses tilt crookedly across his chocolaty brown eyes. He shrugged one shoulder. "I'm definitely not jealous of them." He dropped his snowball on the ground, then shook the excess snow off his gloves. "I'm freezing. I better get inside."

I'm not sure why, but I felt disappointed, even though part of me wanted to go inside too. My ears practically had frostbite, and I could smell the cozy fire from my chimney. I guess I didn't want to go back to my dad's lecture.

I grinned, cocking back my snowball arm. "What's the matter? You chicken? Guess the older brother I never wanted can't take the heat *or* the cold."

I expected Joey to grin back at me. Maybe even joke that I was the little sister *he'd* never wanted. I expected him to lunge at me and knock the snowball out of my hand. But instead he shoved his hands into the pockets of his coat. "*Brother*? I don't think so."

I rolled my eyes. "Okay, fine, cousin, neighbor, whatever."

Joey pursed his lips at me. "Neighbor," he said. "Let's stick with neighbor."

"Neighbor and longtime snowball-fight nemesis!" I shouted, letting my snowball fly right at his head. He easily ducked out of the way. The snowball hit the pavement behind him and splattered.

"Nice try," he said, laughing. "But you'll never ambush me. I know what you're thinking before you do."

"Oh, really?" I arched an eyebrow at him. "So what am I thinking right now?"

Joey's smile spread slowly across his face. "Easy. You're thinking I'll never be able to guess what you're thinking."

"That's so not fair!" I started to shout, but then I heard a knock at the window behind me, and I jumped. It was Papi.

"Shoot! I told my father I'd come right back inside." I wondered how long I'd have to listen to the "don't turn out like your mother" speech. The funny thing was, Papi thought the way to keep me safe was to make sure I went to college and figured out what I wanted to do, but I knew something he didn't know. I'd never turn out like my mother because I was never going to fall in love. If she'd been practical instead of romantic, she'd have saved all of us a whole bunch of trouble. But she was still that way: Every summer when I went to visit her, she was either just beginning a new love or just getting over another broken heart.

"I guess I'll see you later, then." Joey took a step toward his house, giving me a small half wave.

I took a step after him. "Did you want to come in?" I asked. "To my house?"

He wrinkled his eyebrows and tilted his head. "You want me to come over?"

"Why are you acting so surprised? You come over all the time."

He shook his head. "Not lately. Not since you started going to Austen. You'd think we'd see each other *more* often since we're at the same school."

I bit my lip. I guessed it had been a while since we'd hung out. "Yeah," I agreed. "I've been really busy trying to find my place in the new school. But there's no time like the present, right?"

"The present is my favorite time." Joeys smiled mischievously. "Think your dad wants to play Settlers of Catan?"

"I hope so," I said, carefully stepping over a patch of ice on my walkway, leading Joey back to my front door. "It would be a nice change of pace from the whole 'School Is the Most Important Thing' talk he keeps giving me."

"Is he getting on your case about the ABC already?" Joey asked, following me up the steps. "That doesn't start for two weeks."

Every year, the seventh graders at Austen Middle School had to write a business plan and put it into action. The ABC, or Austen Business Challenge, was a big deal. Students actually sold goods and services to other students and staff. All the money went to charity, and the student with the best business got to go to a Future Entrepreneurs conference in Chicago.

"No, thank goodness." I paused with my hand on the front door. "He hasn't mentioned it yet. So don't bring it up, okay?"

Joey held up three fingers. "He won't hear about it from me. Scout's honor."

Then Joey paused on the bottom step of my front porch and looked at me as I started to open the front door. "Just out of curiosity, what kind of business were you thinking of?"

I shrugged. "I don't know. I haven't gotten any ideas yet."

He scrunched up his lips, thinking. "If you wanted, I'd

let you see my business plan from last year. I did pretty okay on it."

"Pretty okay?" I laughed. "I heard you won."

Joey twitched his lips like it was no big deal, but the truth was, I wasn't trying to win. I just wanted to do well enough that Papi didn't freak out and decide he was even more disappointed with me. My main priority was finally having friends. No, not just having friends. Being popular. My whole life, I was a popular girl stuck inside a loser. That was finally starting to change.

"Thanks for the offer," I told Joey, "but I'm sure I'll think of something."

Joey shrugged. "That's cool. The offer's open if you change your mind. What's that?" Joey pointed up at my roof, and when I looked, I felt a spray of snow blast the back of my neck and shoulders

"Joey!" I shrieked, brushing the powdery flakes away with my fingers. "No fair!"

Joey sped past me into the house before I could retaliate.

"Sorry," he said, turning around and waggling his eyebrows at me. "But you're the snowball-fight nemesis I always wanted."

Chapter Three

I looked around the cafeteria as I carried my lunch sack to my seat. It was the first day of second semester, and I still couldn't believe that I was sitting at one of the center tables, the tables that let everyone in the school know that I was one of the people to be seen, and not one of the kids who wished they could disappear. I made sure to keep my shoulders back as I walked, and keep my steps light and smooth. I noticed a group of girls from my gym class watching me as I passed, and I smiled. Not at them, though. I smiled like I was thinking about how my life was cool and amazing and perfect.

Today I had worn my new green ballet flats again, even though Papi said I was an *idiota* and it would be my own fault when my toes fell off from cold. But the green shoes looked the best with the new stretchy jeans that I got for Christmas. Papi also said I was an *idiota* for wanting jeans that cost as much as a car. But every year he let me choose one of my presents for myself, and they didn't *really* cost as much as a car.

I sat down at the corner of the table in between Emily and Alivia and started to unpack my lunch. Danielle and Kacy sat on the other two sides of the square cafeteria table. They were the other two girls in our group. They both played field hockey and soccer with Alivia.

"Which cookies would you rather buy?" Alivia spread four plates of cookies in front of us. We had to inch our lunches out of the way. I could tell from the way she made her voice a bit louder than it needed to be that she was hoping kids at other tables would notice.

I uncapped my thermos of last night's *albondigas* soup and took a big spoonful. I still wasn't sure how much Alivia liked me. She hadn't really spoken much to me until the

21

fourth week of school, when I did her Spanish homework for her one day when she forgot it. It was no big deal. I know Spanish as well as I know English.

"Oh my gosh," Emily gushed. "Those smell so good." She scooted over to make a little more room for me between her and Alivia. There wasn't quite enough space for all five of us. "Are those for your ABC project? I can't believe that starts so soon."

"Yeah." Alivia pulled out her laptop. "I'm doing a pastry shop, and I thought I'd take a survey to see which treats are the most popular."

Alivia had made four kinds of cookies. Chocolate chip. Rainbow confetti. A black-and-white swirly cookie. And one that definitely looked like it had oatmeal in it.

"You're so organized. I can't believe you have this all ready to go on the Monday we're back from break," Danielle said.

Alivia shrugged one shoulder like it was no big deal. "You have to be prepared if you want to win. And I want to win." She pointed to the cookies again. "Which one?"

Danielle broke off a little piece of each kind of cookie and took a taste. "I like the rainbow cookie."

"It looks so good." Emily nodded and picked up a cookie, but put it back on the plate when Alivia bulged her eyes.

I didn't really believe in diets. I thought people were supposed to come in all shapes and sizes, but I guessed a whole cookie was a lot for anyone. Alivia had made really big cookies. I picked up the confetti cookie and broke it in half. I took a bite from one half and gave the other one to Emily.

"I like the oatmeal M&M." Kacy grabbed an entire cookie and took a giant bite.

"Yeah, those look good too," Emily agreed.

Alivia recorded everyone's choices on her laptop. "What about you, Clara?"

"I'd buy the confetti cookie," I said, taking another bite.

Alivia nodded, then swept all the cookies back into a plastic container. Everyone moved their lunches forward on the table to eat normally again.

"Does everyone else know what they want to do for ABC?" Danielle asked. "I can't think of any ideas."

"I don't know what I'm going to do," Emily said. "I'll never be able to run a business by myself."

Alivia zipped a padded case around her laptop, put it in

her backpack, and then pulled out her lunch. "You don't have to do it by yourself, you know," she said as she unwrapped a package of sushi and opened a bottle of sparkling water. "You're allowed to have business partners."

Emily's eyes lit up. "Do you want help? I'd totally do a baking business with you."

Alivia's eyes darted from side to side, and she chewed on her lip. "Oh, I'm sorry, but Kacy and I were talking about working together, right, Kace?"

Kacy made a big show of swallowing the chunk of bagel she'd been chewing. "I'm doing a one-on-one soccer coaching business. I think you meant Danielle."

Alivia smacked her palm against her forehead. "I'm so stupid, that's right. I mean Danielle and I were talking about working together, right, Dan?"

"Absolutely!" Danielle nodded, and I watched Emily's neck break out in red splotches as she blinked real fast a bunch of times and tried to pretend like she believed their conversation.

"I'm sorry, Em," Alivia said, a bit of pink coloring her cheeks too.

"Oh. No problem," Emily said, shaking her head. Her

honey-blond curls shimmered under the cafeteria lights. "I bet you guys will have the best business this year. Those cookies are awesome. I'll definitely buy one. Probably more than one."

"Thanks," Alivia said. "I'm sure your business will be great too."

"You can work with me, Emily." I tilted my thermos to get the last bite of soup. "I don't have a partner yet."

Emily's smile was so big I couldn't decide if I should feel happy or sad for her. Alivia gave me confused look. It made the skin on the back of my neck prickle. I thought she'd be glad I was working with Emily. That way she wouldn't need to feel guilty. Now a part of me wished I could take my offer back.

Emily turned to me, peeling her banana and taking a bite. "I'll help any way you need," she said, chewing. "What kind of business are you doing?"

I twisted the cap on my thermos and dropped it into my lunch bag. Then I bit my bottom lip. It was definitely too late to take my offer back. Besides, I needed the help. "I don't know yet," I told her. "I'm open to suggestions if you have any."

Emily nodded seriously. "I don't have any ideas right now, but I promise I won't stop think—uh, I won't—"

Suddenly Emily's jaw dropped and her neck got even splotchier. The redness crept up her face and into her round, dimpled cheeks.

I turned to see what she was gawking at and watched Evan Cho, one of Joey's friends from Mathletes, walk past our table.

"Seriously?" Alivia unwrapped a straw, stuck it in her water bottle, and took a sip. "Do you *like* him?"

Emily's eyes dropped to her lap, and she started to pick the blue polish off her thumbnail. "I don't know. We take karate together. He's really nice and smart and . . . I mean, what do you guys think of him?"

Kacy shrugged. "Don't know him. He's in eighth grade, right?"

"Doesn't he do that math contest thing?" Danielle asked, wrinkling her nose.

"Is he wearing a math T-shirt?" Alivia said.

"Oh. Um. I don't know." Emily began to peel the polish off her index finger. I looked at Evan. His shirt definitely had math symbols on it.

Dating a math geek seemed like exactly the kind of difference that Alivia had been talking about. I hated to admit it, but Evan was probably not the best guy for Emily to choose if she wanted to stay in the popular group, which she did. Otherwise why would she still be hanging out with us? And I wanted her here too. Without Emily, I didn't know if I would still be part of the group. And being in this group, even though it wasn't perfect, was way better than being a gigantic loser. I knew from experience.

So, if Emily didn't want to be a gigantic loser too, it was basically my duty to help her out. And help myself out.

"I bet I could find the perfect guy for you," I told her, patting her knee.

Emily looked up at me, her eyes wide and blinking. "The perfect guy?"

I nodded. "Just like at the mall. It would be fun, playing Cupid for you." And since *I'd* be finding her match, I could be sure to be practical and not get swept away by romance. Not only would I help Emily find a popular-group-worthy guy, I'd be saving her a lot of heartbreak too.

Kacy crumpled her napkin and tossed it at me. "Hello?

We're in middle school. It's not like she's going to meet the love of her life or anything." She burst out laughing.

Danielle tilted her head thoughtfully. "It's not common, but people definitely can marry someone they dated in middle school."

"No," I said. I didn't want them getting the wrong idea. This was just for fun. Nothing serious. "It wouldn't be like that. Look . . ." I pointed to the red-and-white sign hanging by the door of the cafeteria, then turned to Emily. "The Hot Chocolate Social is in six weeks. Didn't you tell me that everyone is always freaking out about the slow dance? I could help you figure out who to dance with *and* get him to ask you."

Kacy stopped laughing. The Hot Chocolate Social usually only had one slow dance, and every girl at Austen wanted a dance partner, but Emily told me there weren't usually very many couples on the dance floor.

"You could do that?" asked Danielle. "Could you find a guy for *me*?"

"I'll take one, too," Kacy said. "But he has to be tall. I feel weird dancing with someone shorter than me."

The right side of Emily's mouth tugged up in a half smile. "I'm sure she could. You should see her at the mall. She picks two random strangers, and before you know it, they're a couple." Emily turned to me. "You should be a professional Cupid when you grow up."

I thought about Emily's words for a second, and a little tingle danced up my spine. "What if I was a professional Cupid now? I mean, what if that was our business for the ABC? A matchmaking business."

"I'd sign up!" said Danielle.

"Me too," agreed Kacy.

"I love that idea," Emily said enthusiastically. "We could even call it . . . Cupid Clara!"

I smiled, blushing a little. "Well . . . I don't know about *that*," I said. But I couldn't deny that I now actually felt excited for the ABC. If everyone else was as excited as Danielle and Kacy, it might actually be the kind of business that helped me stay popular. Plus I did find matchmaking sort of easy: It was just a matter of seeing who had things in common, and then putting them together. The more I thought about it, the more I realized Cupid Clara—

the name was kind of growing on me—would be a perfect business.

"All right!" I said. "I'll make Emily my test case, and then Danielle and Kacy can be my first customers."

Kacy and Danielle cheered.

Emily sat back in her chair and hugged herself. "I'm so nervous. What if you can't find a guy for me?"

"Don't worry," I said. "I'll definitely be able to find you a guy. You too, Alivia. If you want."

Alivia had been silent this whole time. Now she shook her head and smiled a twinkly eye smile. "Nope," she said. "I already know who I want to dance with."

"Who?" Danielle said.

"You didn't tell us you liked someone." Kacy playfully pushed Alivia's shoulder.

"Do you want me to help fix you up with him?" I asked.

Alivia looked at the ceiling, then burst into giggles. "I think he might like me back already," she said. "But I don't want to talk about it. I really like him. Every time I talk about it, it makes it feel like I might jinx it." Alivia clutched her stomach. "Now I feel totally nauseous."

Danielle patted Alivia's shoulder. "I think you might be in love."

I looked at Alivia and started to feel a little uneasy. If she liked a boy that much, I couldn't help worry she was headed for heartbreak. It was why I was never going to like anyone myself.

"Can't you give us a clue?" Kacy asked.

Alivia carefully screwed the cap back onto her water bottle and stared at all the garbage from her lunch stacked into a tidy little pile. "Nope."

"Don't worry," Emily said. "You don't have to tell us. We understand."

"Oh my gosh," Danielle said. "I just realized how fun the dance is going to be if we have boys to dance with. Clara, you are the best!"

Half of Danielle's words made me feel awesome. This business might be the perfect thing to help me get closer to the rest of the group. But what if *I* didn't want to dance with a boy? How much fun would the dance be for me if I were the odd girl out?

Chapter Four

I dipped the wooden spoon in the pan to take a taste of my rice and beans. *Perfect.* I liked them really spicy. I left the food on the stove with the heat turned all the way down and set the table for two. Whether he was working downtown or in his office at home, Papi always liked for us to eat dinner together at seven thirty. When I was younger, my babysitters would get dinner ready. But I didn't need a sitter every day anymore, so Papi and I shared the job of cooking.

I set out place mats and water glasses, then glanced at the clock. I only had a few minutes left until Papi came home, so I packed up my math book from the kitchen counter and put it away in my backpack.

My dad always wanted me to finish my homework right away after school, but now that I was popular-ish, I had lots of other stuff to do first. I had to help Alivia with her Spanish homework and sometimes her English homework too. And then I needed to check my emails and text with Emily . . . my homework was often an afterthought.

I gently squeezed all the avocados on the counter, and when I found one with the perfect amount of give, I cut it, peeled and sliced it, and set it on a plate with a sprinkle of salt. I was just spooning the rice and beans onto our plates when Papi walked into the kitchen. His hair was mussed and his tie was loose. He looked tired and worn down.

"Is everything okay?" I asked him.

"*Sí*. Smells delicious, Clara," he said, giving me a kiss on my cheek. My father was the only one who pronounced my name *Clah-ra*, to rhyme with *star-a*. Not *Clair-a*, like most people.

I set our plates on the table, and we both sat down.

"So," my father said, spreading his napkin on his lap, "how was school today?"

"Good. I thought of an idea for my ABC project," I said.

"*¡Fantástico!*" Papi finished chewing and set down his fork. "What's your idea?"

"I'm going to run a matchmaking service for the middle school. I really think the other kids will like my business a lot. Emily, Danielle, and Kacy already want to be my customers!" The more I talked the more excited I got. "Everyone is going to be coming to me to find the perfect match. My business could really help me click with people at Austen. If it goes well, I think I'll finally be totally accepted."

Papi wiped his mouth with his napkin and laid it next to his plate. He stared at me for a few seconds, then dragged both hands slowly down the front of his face.

"I don't know, Clara." He shook his head. "This doesn't sound too good."

"Um." I felt like someone had shoved me hard in the chest. My lungs got too tight to breathe properly. I thought my dad would love my business idea. "Wait. What?"

"At your age, you need to be concentrating on school, not boys." My father picked up his water glass and took a big

34

drink. He exhaled a long noisy sigh. "I think your mother might have been right."

"Papi," I said, shaking my head. "You've got it all wrong. I'm not concentrating on boys. I'm starting a *business*. A matchmaking business. I think I'd be good at it. Why are you talking about *Mom*?"

I should have prepared better for this conversation. But I thought Papi would be proud of me. Sometimes it seemed no matter how hard I tried, I was just too much trouble for him.

"Your mother called me today." My father laid a hand on the table. The vein in his forehead started to darken. "She wants you to come live with her. All the time now. She said a girl your age is changing. Needs a *mami* more than a *papi*."

"No," I said. "It's not true. I won't do the matchmaking business if you don't want. I just want to stay here with you."

Papi stared at me. I could hear my words reverberating in my head. I wanted to plead even more, but I didn't want to be a burden on him. My mother's words, the ones she said to me the morning she left, were always at the back of my

35

mind: *"Don't cause Papi any trouble. He needs you to take care of him now."*

Because of that, I'd never really told him about how bad it had gotten for me at my old school, Holy Cross. He'd thought I just wanted a change of scenery. He didn't know that anyone who had to sit next to me would always scoot just an inch or two farther away, like I had some contagious disease. That anyone who had to be my partner would roll their eyes in disgust. He didn't know that making friends at Austen was way more important to me than grades.

He already had enough to worry about: being a single dad and dealing with his sadness over my mother leaving, which never quite went away. He didn't need me to make that worse.

"Clara," Papi said, his eyes dimming. "I love you, but a girl your age . . ."

My father's eyes grew watery, like they did whenever he started thinking about my mother. And like I always did, I pretended things weren't so bad, so he'd feel better.

"I'm the same as I always was," I assured him. "You'll see. Let me prove it to you. And don't send me to live with Mom."

Papi sighed. "Okay, you do your matchmaking business, try harder in school. We'll see how it goes. But your mother wants to talk with you. I want you to listen to what she says."

I exhaled. "I will," I told him. My eyes started prickling, and I could feel the heaviness of tears building up behind them. A lump welled halfway up my throat and then stuck, but I swallowed it away. I couldn't be the loser with good grades anymore, but I couldn't be the popular girl with bad grades either. Not if I wanted to stay at home. I couldn't give Papi any reason not to want me.

On Wednesday, Emily came home from school with me so we could get to work on Cupid Clara. She would be my assistant *and* my first customer.

"Are you sure you don't mind being a guinea pig?" I asked her as we settled down in my room with a plate of orange slices and two bottled waters.

"I don't mind at all," Emily said. "I mean, I know you know what you're doing."

"Great." I twisted the cap on my water and took a sip. "Because having a success story is good for business. Once people see you with your match," I told Emily, "they'll all be racing to sign up."

"This is going to be so much fun," Emily said, biting into an orange wedge. "I can't wait to see who you pair me with."

"Okay, then let's get started. I think the best tool for making this many matches will be a questionnaire, so I wrote us one." I handed Emily the sheet of questions I'd printed. "Why don't you fill it out while I work on the sign for our storefront?"

During the business contest, my school used the big lobby in front of the office as an actual marketplace, and every business that wanted to sell things at school got their own table. You could decorate it however you wanted, but a sign was mandatory. I pulled out a huge stack of red, white, and gold paper, plus cutouts of hearts, cupids, arrows, and mugs of hot chocolate. I was going to collage our sign. I dipped my foam brush in the glue and layered the first strip of paper onto a big wooden heart.

I'd almost forgotten the sweet gluey smell of Mod Podge. I trailed the brush over the top of the paper to seal it. Sofia, my one and only friend at my old school, always giggled at how much I'd liked that smell. We'd both liked doing art projects; it was the one thing we had in common besides being social outcasts. But I hadn't made a collage since the day T. J. Thomson told everyone I had Sofia's snot in my hair. It had really been Mod Podge.

I tore off three more strips of paper and tacked them down quickly. The heart was halfway covered when Emily handed me back her questionnaire.

CUPID CLARA QUESTIONNAIRE

Name: Emily Schmidt

Age: 12

Birthday: September 22

Favorites

Subject in school: math

After-school activity: karate, choir

Hobbies: doing logic puzzles, reading science fiction

Animal: orangutan

Food: spaghetti and meatballs

Dessert: Rice Krispie Treats

Type of music: show tunes

Which do you prefer . . .

Watching movies or TV shows?: movies

Board games or video games?: video games

Being inside or outside?: inside

Random Questions

What are three words you'd pick to describe
yourself?: helpful, friendly, fun

Is the glass half-empty or half-full?: half-full

Why did you cross the road?: Um, I don't know
what this means.

I read it, then tucked it in the red folder I'd bought for
Cupid Clara paperwork. One pocket was full of empty
questionnaires; the other pocket now held Emily's com-
pleted survey.

"Do you think my answers are okay?" she asked me.
"Like, good enough for a match?"

"Of course they're good enough! This isn't about being

good enough or not good enough," I explained. "It's about finding the person whose answers are the most similar to yours. Like if you both prefer watching movies and love Rice Krispie Treats, then you'd probably have fun hanging out together. Make sense?"

"I guess." Emily looked at my half-finished sign. "Want me to help with that?"

"Sure," I said, handing her a brush and a stack of colored paper. I showed her how to lay the glue underneath and on top of the paper, and also how to rip so she'd get a cool jagged white edge on the paper.

"Wow," Emily said after a few minutes. "You're really good at this." She pointed to our sign. "Your side looks like something I could buy in an art gallery, and mine looks like . . . a mess."

"You've just never collaged before." I patted her shoulder with my clean hand. "I've made a million of these, so I know what looks good."

"I didn't know you were into art!" Emily added a gold heart to the collage, then layered a strip of sheer red tissue over half of it.

"That looks good," I told her. "You're getting the hang of it."

"How come you aren't taking art? Or doing art club?" Emily asked. "I'd do it with you if you want."

"Ew!" I said, then I realized how that sounded. "I don't mean *ew* about doing an activity with you. I'm just not *that* into art. Anymore. It was something I used to do. Besides, you and Alivia and everyone do dance and soccer, right? I was thinking I might try out for soccer with you guys this spring."

For a second, I thought Emily looked disappointed. "Oh yeah, sure. I mean, it's more Alivia's and Kacy's thing. I'm not really that good, but I'll try out with you."

"We can practice together. But first, we have to finish this sign." Emily and I got back to work, gluing and talking about other ideas for the business.

Later that night, I wrote up our business plan.

```
                    CUPID CLARA

   A matchmaking business that will help students
   at Austen Middle School find a dance partner
   for the Hot Chocolate Social, and maybe even a
   boyfriend or girlfriend!

      1) Students can fill out questionnaires
   for free.
```

2) We will go through the questionnaires and match students together. If students want to find out who their match is, it costs $5.

3) If students want us to connect them with their match, that will cost an additional $10.

I figured those prices were fair. That way, I could make up to fifteen dollars per customer. It wouldn't be too much work since I'd already prepared the questionnaire. I wouldn't have to keep making more and more baked goods like Alivia, or like the kids who sold jewelry or T-shirts. The only downside was I just didn't know how many customers I'd get. But if I could find the perfect guy for Emily before Monday, I was pretty sure I'd have a line as long as the entire school.

Chapter Five

For the next two days, I took notes on every boy in every one of my classes. I had a couple of ideas, but it was important for Emily's match to be a guy that every girl would drool over. Then they'd all be begging to be a client.

I kept a blank questionnaire with me at all times, just in case. I brought a whole stack of them to Alivia's house on Friday night. Her parents were letting her have the party in their new basement. They just added a Ping-Pong table, a Pop-A-Shot, and a big TV for a home movie theater. They even had a popcorn cart.

Emily and I both got root beers from the mini fridge

and sat in the reclining movie seats. Alivia didn't put on a movie, but she had the top-forty station playing on the TV, so I swung my foot to the beat. Kacy and Savannah, another girl in our grade, played Ping-Pong, and Alivia and Danielle sat at a game table in the corner decorating cookies for later.

Emily tugged at the stretchy pink shirt I'd made her borrow. I grabbed her hand and put it on her lap.

"Stop fidgeting," I told her. "You look gorgeous."

Emily adjusted the shirt one more time and said, "I wish you'd have let me wear my sweatshirt. I don't feel like me."

"This is the *new* you," I told her. Hopefully it was the Emily that fit into the popular group.

"Alivia," Alivia's mom called down the basement stairs. "A few more of your friends have arrived."

Alivia stood up and put the cookies on the counter at the back of the room. Above us, what sounded like a hundred water buffalo tromped down the stairs. It was the guys. I patted the folded questionnaires in my back pocket.

"Where's the food?" Mateo asked as soon as he appeared in the basement.

"You're such a pig," Alivia said, laughing and swatting his shoulder, but then she called up the stairs. "Mom, we're ready for the hors d'oeuvres."

Alivia's mother brought down trays of mini pizzas, soft pretzels, tiny hot dogs, chips, and veggies. Everyone pounced on them like they were starving. I hung back so I could make a mental list of all the boys.

Jack, Ben, and Ryan were the sporty boys.

Connor, Sam, and Miles were the future politicians.

Mateo and Eli were the class jokesters.

And then there was Logan. He was newish at our school, just like me. He'd transferred in October. I think his parents got separated or something. He was standing by the mini pizzas, but he wasn't taking any. His thick brown hair was cut short and neat. But he was cute. And kind of mysterious.

"Be right back," I whispered to Emily. Then I got up and walked over to Logan. The old Clara never would have been able to talk to a boy at a party. First of all, she never would have been invited to the party, and second of all, the boy would have run off in the other direction. But New Clara could talk to anyone, because nobody knew a thing about her past.

"Hi," I said, picking up a plate and serving myself a mini pizza with peppers. This was it. The start of Cupid Clara. My heart was beating so wildly it felt like there was a helicopter in my chest, but I pretended I was practically bored. "What's up?"

"Hey," Logan said, smiling. "Did you try the math homework yet? It's impossible."

"Not yet. Thanks for the tip." I smiled back at him, but not too big. I was feeling pretty good about my choice. Logan had brought up math. Math was Emily's favorite subject. So far so good.

"You look like you are having a hard time deciding," I said, pointing to his empty plate.

His cheeks got a little pink, and he looked down at the ground for a second. "I'm not that hungry actually. I didn't realize this party was going to have food, so I already ate."

"Next time you'll know better," I said, remembering something Emily had told me. "When Alivia throws a party, her mom serves enough food to feed the whole school. They even hire a caterer. Wait until you see the desserts! At her last party, they had a chocolate fountain."

"Whoa!" Logan made an appreciative face.

"Yeah, I know. Chocolate-covered anything is my favorite."

"Me too." Logan smiled at me, and I suddenly remembered that Emily's favorite dessert was Rice Krispie Treats.

"What about Rice Krispie Treats?" I asked. "Do you like them?"

"Who doesn't?" he answered, nodding enthusiastically.

Perfect! That was two things Logan and Emily had in common so far.

Logan was going to be a great match. He was obviously popular, since Alivia had invited him to her party, and judging from how many girls were looking at him, he'd make a solid success story. Everyone would sign up if they thought they could get their own Logan.

"I'm hanging over there with my friend Emily." I pointed across the room to where Emily was sitting on the couch watching us. I waved at her, and she waved back cheerfully, her curls bobbing. "She's so cute, isn't she?"

"Um, I—" Logan's cheeks turned pink again. "Sure," he finally said.

He thought she was cute! All signs were go for a Cupid Clara match. But I didn't want to rush it. I had to do things by the book.

"Can I ask you a favor?" I pulled a Cupid Clara questionnaire out of my back pocket and handed it to him. "You know about the ABC, right? Austen Business Challenge? Well, I'm doing a matchmaking business, and I feel like I know someone perfect for you."

Logan looked me right in the eye and blinked a couple of times in surprise. Then he smiled, first with just half of his mouth, then all the way. "You do?"

"Yeah. It's mostly to find a person to dance with at the Hot Chocolate Social, but you could also ask the person out, if you wanted to."

"Okay." He nodded his head.

"All you have to do is fill out this questionnaire, and I'll let you know if you guys are a match. I'm going to ask all the other boys to do it."

"Hey there! What are you guys talking about?" Alivia walked up to the food table and angled herself right between me and Logan. She grabbed a carrot and took a bite.

"Just the ABC," I told her.

"Cool. Hey, Logan, remember you told me you'd teach me how to play Pop-A-Shot?" Alivia smiled at him.

Logan gave her an embarrassed look, then glanced back at me. "Um, I said would give her some shooting tips."

"Oh. No problem. Go ahead." I held out two questionnaires. "You can give it back to me at school on Monday. Keep the extra for mistakes, or give it to one of your friends."

Logan took the questionnaires and tucked them in his back pocket. I couldn't believe how smoothly everything was falling into place. It's like I was destined to be Cupid Clara. I was helping myself to a mini hot dog and some baby carrots when Mateo came over to me. Suddenly I found it hard to breathe, and a tiny piece of baby carrot went down the wrong pipe and launched a giant coughing fit.

Mateo pounded my back. "Are you okay?"

I took a deep breath. *Remember you're cool now*, I chanted in my head. But it didn't work. I kept coughing, and I could feel myself turning bright red.

Mateo and I had both gone to Holy Cross School together until fifth grade, then he switched to Austen for middle school. One year before me. We weren't friends at Holy

Cross, obviously. He was never mean to me there, but he was never nice either. Now that we were part of the same friend group at Austen, I mostly tried to avoid him. For some reason, whenever I was near him, Old Clara came rushing back and it was impossible to let my inner popular girl out.

"What's up with you and the new kid?" he asked.

I never knew how to act around Mateo. He was always nice to me now, but whenever I spoke to him, I felt like any minute he was going to tell everyone I was an imposter, or make some kind of comment about how I used to be the school outcast.

"Nothing," I said, coughing one last time. "He's just doing something for my ABC project." I thought about handing Mateo a questionnaire, but my nerves failed me.

"Oh," he said, picking up a handful of chips. "Cool."

He popped a chip into his mouth but didn't go anywhere. I got the feeling he wanted to say something to me, but he wasn't speaking. I was about to sit back down with Emily when he finally spoke.

"Do you ever see, um, *anyone* from the old school anymore?" he asked.

I froze. The hair on my arms prickled, and all the noise in the room faded as Mateo came into crystal-clear focus in front of me. He *knew* I only had one friend in elementary school. Why would he ask me that question? Was he getting ready to do something mean? In front of everyone?

A surge of energy filled my body. There was no way I was going to let him do that.

I put my plate down and stared right into his eye. "I never even think about that school anymore," I told him. My voice was shaking. Then I spun around and walked away from him as fast as I could.

In second grade, I was the girl who cried during recess. In third grade, I was the liar who tried to claim her mother was a movie star. By fourth, fifth, and sixth grade, it didn't matter who I was anymore because all anyone remembered was second and third grades. But in seventh grade, I started over. Now I'm the new Clara, the girl who's practically popular. I'm not going to let that change.

Chapter Six

On Monday after school, I walked outside with my friends and nearly froze to death. It couldn't have been warmer than negative two degrees outside, but Alivia wasn't even wearing her coat. Danielle and Kacy had their coats half on, half off.

"It's freezing!" Emily shrieked, pulling her hat and scarf from her bag and putting them on. Her coat was zipped up to her chin.

"Emily!" Alivia said shaking her head. "Your hair's going to look crazy at dance when you take that off."

Emily's pink cheeks got even pinker, and she reached her hand up to her head, then put it back down.

I had started zipping my coat, but I stopped and wrapped my arms around myself instead. At that moment, Joey walked out the side door of the school. Even though he was half the school away, I could tell it was him by the way he walked. I watched him out of the corner of my eye as he put on his pom-pom ski cap and big woolly mittens and wrapped an extra-long striped scarf around and around and around his neck.

Alivia laughed. "Don't look now, Clara, but I'm pretty sure I see the guy you've been looking for."

Suddenly I didn't feel cold at all. My cheeks burned a thousand degrees and my neck began to sweat. "What are you talking about?"

"Aren't you looking for a match for Emily?" She laughed again and pointed at Joey. "Don't you think they'd be perfect all bundled up together?"

Emily looked at me uneasily. I didn't know what to say.

"I'm just kidding," Alivia said.

I thought about mentioning Logan's questionnaire. He'd slipped it through the vents of my locker. When I packed up my bag after school, I'd found it next to a smushed pack of Reese's Peanut Butter Cups I didn't know I had. But I decided not to say anything. It would be a better surprise that way.

"Hey, Clara!" Joey called. I shifted from foot to foot but didn't turn around. I pretended I didn't hear him.

"I was thinking I might sign up for dance with you guys next session," I said.

"Clara!" Joey shouted again.

"I think that guy's calling your name," Danielle told me.

"Oh." I turned around and waved to Joey. "Hey," I said.

"Do you want me to wait for you to walk home?" Why was he talking so loudly? I could feel Alivia's eyes poking the back of my head.

"That's okay," I answered. "I'm good."

"Okay, see you." Joey waved good-bye but then went back into school again.

I turned back to the group to see four pairs of eyes staring at me.

"Who was that?" Kacy asked.

I waved my hand in the air like I was waving Joey away. "Just my next-door neighbor," I said.

"Do you *like* him?" Emily asked, a sweet smile sneaking up one corner of her mouth.

"Joey?" I shook my head. Hard. "Definitely not. I've known him since we were babies."

"Who *do* you like?" Alivia asked, tilting her head at me.

I shrugged. "No one."

Alivia raised one eyebrow at me, like she didn't believe what I was saying.

"Really," I said.

"Well, who would you want to dance with at the Hot Chocolate Social?" Danielle asked.

"I don't know. Seriously. I make matches for other people, not for myself."

"I saw you talking with Logan and Mateo at Alivia's party," Kacy pointed out.

"But not because I like them!" I held both hands in the air as if I were at gunpoint.

Just then, Alivia's mom pulled up in her giant black SUV. Thank goodness. I waved good-bye to my friends as they climbed inside, and then I scurried across the school yard.

When I reached the corner, I stopped, shivered, and looked around. Alivia's car was nowhere in sight, so I zipped up my coat and pulled my earmuffs out of the front pouch of my backpack. By that point, I was so cold it barely mattered.

"I guess you're the one who waited for me," Joey's voice said behind me.

I turned to look at him. "I'm definitely not waiting for you." I hoisted my backpack back over one shoulder, but then I really did wait for him to catch up.

"Oh, that's right," he said, falling in step beside me. "I forgot. When we're at school, you have to pretend you don't know me."

I gave him a sideways wrinkled-eyebrow look. "I don't have to pretend I don't know you!"

He clapped his gloved hand to his heart. "Then it's even worse than I thought. You *choose* to pretend you don't know me. The math geek next door: You'll talk to him only if no one else is around."

"You're not a math geek!" I protested, but then I blushed because that was exactly how Alivia and a lot of other people at Austen actually saw Joey. "They just don't know you. You're cool. And I never even see you at school. Hardly ever anyway. We're in different grades."

"First of all, you don't have to lie to make me feel better. I am a math geek *and* I'm cool. I'm just not the right kind of cool for you and your friends." Joey bumped shoulders with me as we walked. I couldn't tell if it was on purpose or by accident. "I see *you* at school all the time. It's weird how you're never looking in my direction."

Joey and I turned the corner onto our street, and I couldn't meet his eyes. I stared up at the ice-coated tree branches. It's possible I'd pretended not to see him once or twice. But it wasn't because I didn't want to talk to him. I just didn't want my friends to get the wrong idea.

"Sorry," I mumbled. Then I turned to face him as we walked. "Here, I'll look at you now to make up for it." Joey turned to me too, shaking his head in a pretend exasperated way, and for the first time, I noticed how long his eyelashes were. And how soft they looked. Like paintbrushes.

And then I stepped on a patch of ice that I didn't see because I wasn't looking at the sidewalk, and I slipped and nearly fell.

"Whoa!" I screamed, arms flailing. Joey grabbed me and held me up while I steadied my feet.

"Are you okay?" he asked.

Even in the cold, I could feel the heat of my blush from my cheeks all the way down my neck. "That was your fault," I said.

"Right," he agreed, nodding. "I made it snow, then I made it melt a little bit and freeze again so there would be ice right there."

He gestured to the ice on the ground with his head, and I realized he had to use his head because both his arms were still wrapped around me! Why were his arms still wrapped around me?

I straightened up, and he let go. We started walking again. "It's your fault because you made me look at you," I explained.

He clasped both hands behind his back under his backpack. I called that his lawyer walk. He only did it when he was trying to prove a point. "You were looking at me because you felt guilty about the way you ignore me at school. So really, it's your fault."

"I don't ign—" I started to say, but stopped when a yellow Holy Cross van drove by us. I could see Sofia in the window, but she was looking straight ahead. I could tell she had seen us, though. It's pretty obvious when someone is only pretending they can't see you.

I looked at Joey, glad he couldn't read my thoughts. I didn't need him to point out the irony.

The van stopped a couple houses up ahead, and Sofia climbed out.

"Hey, Sof!" Joey called out.

She turned and waved at him. I wasn't sure what I should do, so by the time I waved too, Sofia had already turned back toward her house and didn't see me.

"Man." Joey whistled. "You guys don't even say hello to each other anymore?"

"It's not like that," I said. "I just go to a different school now."

"I used to go to a different school from you, and we talked all the time."

"Sofia and I grew apart." Sort of. Sofia and I were never really that close, despite being each other's only friends.

Joey and I walked past Sofia's house, almost to the end of our block. He didn't say anything the whole rest of the way, and I knew it was because he didn't believe me.

When we got to our driveway, Joey kept walking toward his front door. For some reason, I didn't want us to go inside our own separate houses with the whole Sofia conversation being the last thing we talked about. Thinking about it made my breath come in short puffy gasps that looked like tiny clouds floating up from my mouth.

"Oh! I forgot to tell you," I said, and Joey turned around. Instantly my breath calmed down.

"I thought of my business."

"What did you pick?" he asked. "Jewelry making? Lemonade stand?"

I shook my head. "I'm going to do a matchmaking business. To help people figure out who they should dance with at the Hot Chocolate Social."

Joey tilted his head at me, and the winter sunlight made his eyes look like amber. "Call me crazy," Joey said, "but shouldn't everyone dance with the person they *feel* like dancing with?"

"You just gave me the best idea!" I swung my bag to the ground, rummaged through it until I found my red folder, and handed Joey a questionnaire. "Fill this out, and I'll tell you who your match is!"

He took the questionnaire but shook his head. "I don't need help figuring out who I like," he told me, glancing over the sheet. "Besides, do you really think liking the same food means two people would like each other?"

I zipped my backpack and swung it back up on my shoulder. "I do," I said, "and I'm going to prove it. I'm about to get to work on my first match right now. When you see how happy they are, you are definitely going to change your mind. Don't worry. I won't rub it in. I'll even give you a discount."

"Your middle name is Crazy, isn't it?" He folded his questionnaire, stuck it in his back pocket, and walked inside. "Clara Crazy Martinez," I heard him mumble just before his door slammed shut.

I shivered, then raced into my own house. I couldn't wait to match Logan and Emily. Cupid Clara was going to be the best business ever.

Chapter Seven

I grabbed a handful of tortilla chips from the kitchen, then raced up to my room to get started. I settled onto my bed, pulled the red Cupid Clara folder from my backpack, and a tingle rushed up my arms. This felt so different from matching random strangers at the mall. It was real. It mattered. I opened the folder and pulled out Logan's questionnaire. It was creased in a couple of places from how he had folded it, so I smoothed it against my bedspread and began reading.

Name: Logan MacClean

Age: 12

Birthday: September 21

Favorites

Subject in school: gym

After-school activity: basketball, baseball

Hobbies: Basketball and baseball. I already told you!

Animal: my dog, Prince—he's a chocolate lab.

Food: steak

Dessert: Reese's Peanut Butter Cups and anything with peanut butter and chocolate!

Type of music: whatever's on the radio and is good

Which do you prefer . . .

Watching movies or TV shows?: TV show

Board games or video games?: video games, as long as they're sports video games

Being inside or outside?: outside

Random Questions

What are three words you'd pick to describe yourself?: athlete, tall, boy

Is the glass half-empty or half-full?: huh?

Why did you cross the road?: to shoot hoops

When I got to the end of Logan's questionnaire, my eyes raced back to the top so I could read it again. I couldn't believe it. I really thought he'd have more in common with Emily. I pulled *her* questionnaire out of the Cupid Clara folder and laid it next to Logan's just in case my memory wasn't working too well.

But when I looked back and forth at their answers, *my* answer was clear.

Logan and Emily weren't a perfect match.

My heart sank to the level of my belly button. I'd been so sure Logan was right for Emily that I didn't pass out any other questionnaires. And now there wasn't enough time to find a different guy for her before the ABC started. Besides, there wasn't really anyone else I knew that seemed right for her. If I didn't match Emily with someone cool, Alivia's prediction about their friendship might come true. And where would that leave me?

Not to mention the fact that if I didn't do a good job on my business, that would affect my report card. And I might not even be going to Austen Middle School anymore. Papi might decide I was too much trouble to take care of. I didn't want to move in with my mother and start at a new school!

I stood up and began to pace back and forth around my room. To make a match, I needed to get a handle on the basic facts. To go over everything I knew about Logan and Emily and human nature.

I sat down and made a list.

BASIC FACTS

1. Logan would like to find a crush. I could tell from the excitement in his eyes when I told him I would find him a match.

2. Emily trusts my opinion.

3. Middle school romances don't last forever anyway.

I didn't love it, but the basic facts seemed to point in a very clear direction. If I told Emily and Logan that they were perfect for each other, they'd believe me. At least long enough for Alivia to see that Emily was cool and for customers to know that Cupid Clara worked. So they'd probably break up eventually, but that was likely to happen anyway, and if they'd never been right for each other in the first place, the breakup wouldn't hurt so badly. I was actually doing them a favor.

Plus this would be a real test of my matchmaking skills. It was one thing to match up two people who were obviously going to like each other, but only a true matchmaker could fix up people that didn't have much in common.

Everyone thought that people had to have some kind of magical sparkle or connection, but attraction was scientific; it was chemicals in the brain. I just had to make the right suggestions here or there, and let chemistry take care of the rest.

It wasn't a perfect match, but it was an okay match. And once they were broken up, I'd find each of them a new, better match and middle school would continue on happily ever after, at least till the end of the school year.

At school the next morning, I was so distracted, I had to redo my locker combination five times before it opened. I was still formulating my plan for how exactly to get Emily and Logan together. I couldn't decide if I should drop hints myself, or if I should make it seem like they already liked each other. Finally my fingers were able to twist the lock without fumbling, and a red piece of paper that had been stuck in my locker vents fluttered to the ground by my feet.

I picked it up and unfolded it. The border of the paper was lined with sticks of gum in shiny silver wrappers. In the center, someone had typed up a message.

I hear you're starting a matchmaking business.
Here's something for you to "chew" on:
Whenever we're together, I hope you "stick" around.
Talking to you makes my heart expand like a bubble.
You should know that YOUR match is walking these halls, waiting for you to realize that we were "mint" to be together like gum on the sole of a shoe.
(Okay, maybe that doesn't sound so great. We really belong together like peanut butter and chocolate, but the Reese's Cups get smushed when I put them through your locker.)

When I finished reading the note, my heart was slamming around inside my chest as though someone was bashing it like a piñata. I looked up and down the hallway, trying to figure out who sent the note and if it was a big joke. If *I* was the big joke.

The hall was crammed with people, everyone grabbing their things out of their lockers before the first bell rang. Nobody seemed to be looking in my direction at all, let alone pointing, laughing, or flashing me cruel smiles.

I read the note again. It was kind of goofy, but it sounded real. Like there was actually a boy in this school who *liked* me. My heart stopped slamming and instead started dancing a crazy fast rhythm. A tiny smile tugged at the corners of my mouth. Somebody liked me? I folded the note back up, put it in my backpack, and then I shut my locker and spun around, feeling like a princess on my way to a royal ball.

Then, suddenly, thank goodness, I came to my senses. A princess? I was ridiculous. This was why I was never going to let myself get swept away by my feelings. I didn't even know who'd sent me the note or if it was real. It could turn out to be a joke after all, or it could be from someone completely wrong for me. Besides, even if it was from a perfect match, I wasn't interested in having a boyfriend. So it didn't matter.

A crush couldn't find me if I wasn't looking. I was the matchmaker, the Cupid launching the arrows. I was *not* the target. I took a deep breath and made a pledge to myself as I walked to science. *No* boyfriends.

Later that morning, someone tapped my shoulder as I was walking from gym to math. I turned to my left, and there was Mateo, matching my pace. His cheeks were bright red.

"Hi, Clara," he said, his face getting even redder.

"Hi," I said, confused. Mateo and I had talked a couple of times when we were hanging out as one big group, but he had never tried to walk with me one-on-one in the hallway before. "What's up?"

"I wanted to ask your advice about something," he said, looking down at the ground.

We stopped in front of my math classroom. We still had a minute or two until the bell would ring, so I didn't go inside. "Okay, what is it?" I asked.

He looked up and down the hallway, then brushed the hair out of his eyes. "Um, it's kind of a secret. I don't want anyone to know just yet. It would be embarrassing if anyone found out."

"I won't tell anyone," I said, but I was curious. Mateo was one of the coolest guys in our grade. What could *he* have to be embarrassed about?

"I don't want to talk about it at school. Maybe I could text you?"

"Sure," I said, starting to feel exasperated. Why didn't he just text me to begin with?

A huge smile of relief burst across Mateo's face. "Thanks," he said. "You're the best."

I walked into math class shaking my head. So far this had been the weirdest morning of my life. I sat down in my seat and pulled out all the budgeting worksheets we'd had to fill out for the ABC, when Logan flopped down into the chair next to me.

"Did you find my thing in your locker?" he asked, pulling out his math folder.

"Your thing?" What was he talking about? The note? *¡Dios mío!* Was he trying to tell me he was my secret admirer? This was terrible! "What thing?" I asked, my voice wobbling.

"You know, my questionnaire." Logan nodded his head encouragingly. "You said you were going to find me a match."

Right! He was talking about his questionnaire. I was going crazy. Of course Logan wasn't crushing on me. He was just after me about his future crush. I took a deep breath. "Oh, yeah, I got it. Thanks."

"So who's the lucky girl?" He chuckled at his own joke.

"I'm still working on it," I told him just as the bell rang and Mr. Bersand asked if anyone was willing to let him put their budget up on the Smart Board as a case study. A girl named Kate raised her hand, and I tried to pay attention to what Mr. Bersand was telling us about the difference between fixed costs and variable costs, but my mind kept drifting back to the secret admirer note.

When math class ended fifty minutes later, I was still in a daze. As I walked out the door, I grabbed the note from my backpack and shoved it to the bottom of the garbage can. I wasn't going to let a tiny piece of paper take over my brain.

Chapter Eight

The next morning, I slid into my seat in science one second before the bell rang. Luckily my seat was next to Emily, and she was the one person I really wanted to talk to.

Mrs. Fox, our science teacher, told us to get out our binders since we were going to watch a video and she wanted us to take notes. The video was all about some guy who grew peas and tried to see if he could make the flowers and peas be a certain color. It was hard for me to pay attention because Emily and I had a lot to discuss.

"I found him!" I whispered as soon as the classroom got

dark. I was moving ahead with my plan of action to convince both Logan and Emily that they'd be perfect for each other. That way, when they found I'd matched them, they'd only see what they expected to see.

"You found who?" Emily asked, eyes wide and confused.

"Your match," I explained. "Your slow-dance dream guy."

Emily started to squeal but quickly covered her mouth with her hand so it sounded like a squeak. Even so, Mrs. Fox made an announcement from the back of the room, "There shouldn't be any talking right now. I want to see pencils moving."

Okay, fine, I thought. *We'll take this old school.* I turned to a blank page of loose-leaf at the back of my binder and wrote a note for Emily at the top.

You both like math, and he loves Rice Krispie Treats too.

That part, at least, was true. I quietly tore the page from my notebook, folded it, and passed it to Emily. She read it, wrote an answer, then checked the back of the room about a hundred times to make sure Mrs. Fox wasn't looking at us before she passed it back. I guessed she didn't know the first rule of note passing. The more you look at the teacher, the more likely they are to look at you.

I opened the note back up.

What else? Tell me EVERYTHING we have in common!!!

I knew she was going to ask that question, and I was prepared. There weren't many things, but there were enough. And besides, I reminded myself, just about anyone could like anyone. If I told them they were perfect for each other, they'd start seeing evidence for that everywhere.

He also loves video games and his birthday is in September. September 21, the day before you!

I casually tossed the note back onto Emily's desk, and she tore into it. Then she read it for a really long time. Like, way longer than it should take to read two sentences. So long I almost started to pay attention to the movie. They were talking about some kind of special squares that you filled up with capital and lowercase letters. It looked confusing, and I realized I was going to have to study extra hard tonight to figure out what those were because they seemed exactly like the sort of thing a teacher would put on a test.

Finally Emily wrote something else and passed the note back to me. She didn't even look around when she passed it.

Who is he?

I scribbled the answer.

Logan MacClean. I talked to him about you at Alivia's party.

Emily again read the note about a million times before she replied.

Are you sure he'd like me? He seems so
He seems more like the kind of guy who'd like someone … cooler.

I wished Emily could see how awesome she was. But maybe having a guy like Logan by her side would be just the thing to show her.

He told me at Alivia's party that he thinks you're cute!

This time when Emily read my note, she looked at me in disbelief. I nodded at her so she'd know it was true. And it was! I'd asked Logan if he thought she was cute and he'd totally said yes. Emily bit her lip and smiled.

"Both our labs this week will be on material related to this video," Mrs. Fox announced to the class, or maybe just to me and Emily. "I sincerely hope you are paying attention."

But I could never go talk to him.
I'd be scared out of my mind!

I read Emily's note and smiled. I knew she would say that and I'd come prepared. Actually I wanted her to say that. It gave me a chance to work on part two of my business.

> Don't worry! You don't have to talk to him at all.
> You can hire me to be your matchmaker, and I'll do
> all the work to get you guys together.
>
> Cupid Clara to the rescue!

I passed the note to Emily just as Mrs. Fox turned the lights back on in our classroom. Whoa. I had missed the entire movie. And I'd been planning on paying attention after that last note too. Oops.

"For tonight's homework, I want a one-page paper explaining Mendel's experiments and then thinking about a trait you have and where it might have come from," Mrs. Fox announced. "Any questions?"

I thought about raising my hand and asking her if she would summarize the whole video for me, but Mrs. Fox was one of those teachers who'd probably give me extra homework if I did something like that.

The bell rang, and Emily grabbed my arm as I walked toward the door of the classroom.

"I'm so nervous," she said. "Do you really think this whole thing will work? I never would have thought to go for a guy like him."

I boinged one of Emily's loose blond curls. "Trust me," I told her. "You're going to have the best Hot Chocolate Social ever."

Emily giggled nervously as we walked into the hallway.

"I'll see you at lunch?" she asked.

"I might be a few minutes late," I told her, patting the front pouch of my backpack. "I've got some Cupid Clara business to take care of."

Logan's locker was, thankfully, far from the cafeteria. Not too many people hung around there when it was lunchtime. I hid in the doorway of one of the classrooms until the hallway was completely empty. Then I pulled the handmade heart-shaped card out of the front pouch of my backpack. It had taken me an hour to make, placing layer after layer of tissue and then sandwiching them between two cardboard heart-shaped frames. It looked like rainbow stained glass. I hadn't meant to spend so much time on it. I'd barely had time to finish my math homework. But the heart *was* for Cupid Clara, which was also a school project.

This morning, when I was sure the glue on the tissue was dry, I wrote a message in fancy lettering.

Roses are red
Violets are blue
Cupid Clara says
I'm the girl for you!
XO,
Your Secret Match
P.S. I'll be at the basketball game tomorrow after school.
Can you guess who I am?

Using removable tacky dots, I stuck the heart on the front of Logan's locker. At first, I was going to slide it through the vents, but then I thought it would be much better for my business if everyone saw the Cupid Claragram (that's what I decided to call it).

When it was done, I took a step back, admiring my work. It looked great.

I had an extra bounce in my step as I turned to walk down the hall and nearly had a heart attack when Logan tore around the corner and nearly knocked me over.

"Hey!" I shouted, picking my bag up off the floor.

"Sorry!" Logan picked up a couple pens that had flown out of my front pocket and handed them to me. "I'm late for lunch because I had to get extra help in language arts and my mom made me bring a lunch today." Logan scowled. "So I had to come all the way to my locker to get it even though LA is right next to the cafeteria."

"That's okay. I'll see you in the caf." I started walking off quickly when Logan said, "Hang on a second. I'll walk with you."

"Um, okay." It might give me a chance to talk up Emily some more.

I stayed where I was and watched Logan jog to his locker. He stared at the heart for a second before looking at me and smiling. Then he opened his locker, grabbed his lunch, and jogged back to me.

"So, Cupid Clara found me a match, huh? Who is it?"

I nodded. "She's great! One of my *favorite* people."

He smiled again. "Mmm-hmm. Any chance you're going to tell me her name?"

I shook my head. "Not yet. You'll just have to deal with your curiosity for now."

Logan laughed and shoved my shoulder. "That's not fair!" he said as we walked into the cafeteria.

I rubbed the bone where he hit me. Ow. Maybe Cupid Clara could also give boys tips on things *not* to do when they are hanging out with girls.

"Oh, look, there's Emily!" I said when I spotted her waving to me from across the cafeteria. "She's the best. I love hanging out with her."

"Cool," said Logan. "She seems nice."

"Sooo nice! And fun. And cute. So, I'll see you later?"

Logan nodded. He started walking toward the table with his friends, then he stopped. "Hey! Are you coming to my game tomorrow?"

I nodded. "I'll definitely be there. I'm going with *Emily*."

Logan's smile stretched practically all the way across the cafeteria. "Cool," he said again. "See you there."

Chapter Nine

Seventh-grade basketball games weren't as crowded as eighth-grade basketball games, but there were still plenty of people packing into the gym when Emily and I arrived.

"Come on. Let's go watch your future dance partner." I took her hand and started pulling her toward the bleachers.

Emily grabbed her hand away and blurted, "I have to go to the bathroom." She raced off before I could stop her.

I threaded my way through the crowd and found Emily staring into the mirror in the bathroom of the girl's locker room.

"You look awesome, Em," I told her. "You know, you totally could have started a hairstyling business."

"Do you really think so?" Emily asked, checking her hair. She'd braided two sections down the back of her head so that her hair was half up, half down.

"Absolutely! You look like a medieval princess." I couldn't believe how good her hair turned out. "You should wear it like that all the time."

Emily wrinkled her nose. "This is how I wore it when I went to my uncle's wedding last summer. Doesn't it seem silly to wear such a fancy hairstyle to a basketball game?" She twisted her dress around at her waist. "Plus this itches and *no one else* is wearing a dress."

"I'm wearing a dress," I reminded her. I wanted Emily to look her absolute best for Logan, and I'd figured it would make more sense if we were both dressed up. "Trust me. You look awesome."

Emily bit her bottom lip, and a little crease appeared between her eyebrows. "Okay," she said. "I'll trust you, but I still feel stupid. It would have made more sense to wear my Austen Middle School sweatshirt."

"Come on." I led Emily back out the door. "Let's go watch the game."

It was already the start of the second quarter when we

arrived in the gym, and the bleachers were pretty packed. I figured it didn't matter too much that we were late, since Logan wouldn't even know if we were there. But as we climbed to our seats, even though he was in a huddle with the coach and the rest of the team, Logan made eye contact with me, then pointed at the giant clock above the basket. He raised one eyebrow at me, as if teasing me for being late. I raised both palms up to the sky and shrugged.

That was a good sign. He was probably really excited to find out who his match was.

"Doesn't he look cute in his basketball uniform?" I asked Emily.

"Uh-huh," she nodded. "So cute."

I headed to an empty spot at the top of the bleachers but stopped when I saw Alivia, Kacy, and Danielle.

"Hey, you guys," I said. "I didn't know you were coming!"

"Didn't I tell you?" Alivia asked. "I'm sorry. I guess I forgot."

"That's okay. We're here now," I said. "Can we sit with you?"

Alivia nodded and slid down the bench and so did Kacy and Danielle.

"Why are you guys so dressed up?" Kacy asked.

I gave her a mysterious smile. "It's a Cupid Clara thing."

Alivia shot me a curious look. "A Cupid Clara thing that has to do with basketball?"

"With a certain basketball player," I said, wagging my eyebrows. But Alivia must not have been able to hear me over the crowd because she turned back to the game and didn't answer.

For the next forty-five minutes, Emily and I cheered as Austen Middle School battled our biggest rival, Brighton Middle School. With less than a minute to go, the score was tied. Logan scored a game-winning basket just before the final buzzer.

Emily and I both leapt to our feet and cheered.

Alivia stood up and clapped too. Then, when the cheering died down, said, "I didn't know you guys were such big basketball fans."

"We're not," I said, smiling. "That was just really exciting."

Alivia tilted her head at me, like I was speaking in some secret code she was trying to understand.

"Should we go wait in the hallway to tell the guys 'good game'?" I asked.

"Sure," she said.

We all walked out of the gym, but instead of turning right and going home, like everyone else, we went left and stood opposite the doors of the boys' locker room.

I was hoping it wouldn't take too long for the players to come out so I could get this fix-up over with. My plan was to pull Logan and Emily aside and tell them they were a match right away. Then I'd give them some time alone. I had to get home and catch up on my science anyway. Plus I still had all my other homework, and it was my turn to cook dinner tonight. If I started ordering out on my days, Papi might think I couldn't handle everything in my life right now. And even though my father hadn't mentioned my mother's plan again since the other night, that would probably be the first thing out of his mouth.

I was running through my mental cookbook, when I heard Emily let out a tiny gasp. I looked up and saw Joey and Evan walking right toward us.

"Hey, Clara," Joey said. "What are you doing here? I thought the only sport you could stand to watch was Ping-Pong."

I stood up straighter, away from the wall, and noticed

Alivia scanning Joey from head to toe. She leaned over to Kacy and whispered something.

I turned my body sideways so I couldn't see Alivia and Kacy, and said, "What are *you* doing here? You're not the world's biggest basketball fan either."

"We just had a math tournament," he said. "We crushed it, and Evan rocked the lightning round."

"That's awesome!" Emily gave Evan a high five. "I can't believe you guys can solve problems in your head so fast. I'd be super nervous."

"You'd be great at it," Evan said.

"We always need more members if you guys want to give it a try." Joey gestured to me and Emily. Behind me, I was certain Alivia was still watching me, and probably wondering if I wanted to be a Mathlete.

"Actually I've always wanted to try it," Emily said. Then she glanced back at Alivia and looked at the ground. "But, um, I don't know."

"We're both kind of busy right now," I said, then I just stood there awkwardly for a second. A mental earthquake was splitting my brain into pieces. Part of me wanted Joey to leave as quickly as possible. Logan was about to come out, and I didn't want him to see Emily hanging out with other guys. But I also didn't want Joey to feel like I was embarrassed to talk to him. Even though I knew Alivia and Kacy were thinking all kinds of mean things about him. I wanted to crawl out of my skin. If only there was a real earthquake. It would be nice to be swallowed up by the ground right about now.

I was frantically trying to think of something to do when I heard somebody shout my last name.

"Martinez!"

Logan bounded over to where I stood with Emily, Joey, and Evan, little drops of water spraying from his freshly showered hair and landing on my face. I tried to wipe them off my cheek without being too obvious about it. Joey didn't try to be subtle. He picked up the edge of his T-shirt and wiped his whole face. He gave Logan a disgusted look too.

"Refreshing," Joey said sarcastically.

I tried to swallow my laugh.

"Hi, Logan." Alivia came and stood right next to me. "Great game."

"Thanks," he said, barely looking at her. Then he turned to me. "You came! I was starting to worry."

"Oh, Emily and I had to take care of something first, but of course we came!" I took a tiny step backward as I spoke and pushed the small of Emily's back so she'd take a step forward. I wanted her to be the most featured girl in Logan's vision.

"What did you think of the final shot?" Logan asked me, peering around Emily.

"They should always pass to you at the buzzer," Alivia said. "You were so calm, you seemed like you were taking a practice shot."

"You were great," I agreed. "Emily, what did you think?"

"Oh, um, it was super exciting." Emily's pale skin turned fiery red. She almost looked like she was breaking out in hives. Her eyes kept darting back and forth between Logan and Evan. "I'd be so nervous having all that pressure on me. Doesn't it freak you out?" Emily said. I wasn't sure which boy she was talking to.

Evan wasn't either, because he started to say, "You get used to it," but Logan cut him off.

"I don't have time to be nervous during a game. I stay in the moment and do what I have to do. But it did help knowing there was a girl in the stands I was trying to impress. I'd have to say that shot was for her!"

I reached behind Emily's back and squeezed her arm where no one could see. Alivia moved to stand by the drinking fountain, and she looked kind of upset. Joey kept looking back and forth between me, Logan, and Emily like we were a particularly fascinating math problem.

"Whoever she is, she's one lucky girl!" I squeezed Emily's arm again. "Don't you think so, Emily?"

"Oh, um, yeah." Emily nodded, the red skin spreading down her neck. "So lucky."

"Evan and I are heading over to Scooper Dooper. Do you want to come?" Joey asked me, breaking into the conversation. Talk about terrible timing. I was just about to suggest Logan, Emily, and I go have a talk in the parking lot. I pressed my lips together and gave him a serious look.

"What?" Joey shrugged.

"Hey! The team is going there too," Logan said, punching my shoulder. "You should come."

"I have a lot of homework," I told him. "I'm not sure."

"Come on," Logan said. "Emily wants you to go with us. Right, Emily?"

Emily's face practically turned purple. Her eyes bulged like a teacher had just called on her but she couldn't remember the question.

"I really think you should come, Clara," Emily squeaked. Then she leaned forward and whispered under her breath. "Please."

I really wanted Emily and Logan to have some time alone. But if Emily was too freaked out to talk to him, then being at Scooper Dooper together wouldn't do any good. And thanks to Joey and Evan, I couldn't do my big reveal just yet. I'd have to go along if I wanted Cupid Clara's first match to be a success. I guessed my other homework would have to wait.

"Okay," I said. "If you guys insist."

Two minutes later, a group of about ten of us headed out the gym doors of the school and down the icy sidewalk. Joey and Evan walked a lot faster than our huge mob, and pretty soon they were way ahead of us. Part of me felt relieved that they weren't still trying to hang with us, but another part of me wanted to catch up with them and apologize. I wasn't even sure what for.

I tried to keep myself one step ahead of Logan and Emily, but every time I went a little faster, they matched my speed. Finally I gave up and fell into step beside them. Alivia sped up and joined us too.

"That was so weird," she said to Logan. "What was with those math guys?" Her voice carried in the freezing air. I hoped Joey couldn't hear her. "They were totally acting like their math contest was the same as playing a basketball game."

Logan laughed. "Foul! Illegal use of the decimal point."

Alivia cracked up at his joke. I wanted to tell them all that even with half a brain Joey would be smarter than they'd ever be, but I kept my mouth shut. Even now, when I was New Clara, the idea of being one versus an entire group was enough to make my throat dry up and my heart start racing.

I checked the time on my phone. It was already five thirty. I had time for thirty minutes of matchmaking at the ice-cream shop and then I'd head home to start dinner and homework.

"So, Logan," I said, moving to avoid an icy patch on the sidewalk, which also made it so that Emily was walking between us, "are you liking Austen Middle School so far?"

He nodded. "It's a lot bigger than my old school, but that's cool. It makes it easier to meet people."

"Do you like everyone you've met so far?" I asked.

"It's hard to tell," he said. "It hasn't really been that long, but the guys on the team seem great. And the girls are really nice."

Emily slipped when he said that, and Logan shot out an arm and grabbed her by the elbow, steadying her. "Careful!" he said.

Hmmm. Physical contact. I took that as a sign. I was going to be bold. "Do you have any guesses about who your secret match might be?"

"Secret match?" Alivia asked.

"Yeah," Logan told her. "I filled out one of Clara's questionnaires, and she's going to find me the perfect girl." Logan bent forward and looked at me around Emily. "I might have a guess who she is," he told me. "I think I'm walking with her right now, actually."

"Oh," Alivia said. "Cool." Her voice didn't sound like she thought it was that cool, though. She slowed her steps and soon was walking with the group behind us. I wondered if she was upset that I'd kept my plans a secret. Cupid Clara was supposed to be confidential, but maybe I could give her a few hints when I found matches for Kacy and Danielle.

But first I had to match Emily. I secretly reached down and squeezed Emily's hand again. She squeezed back.

"I can't say yes or no," I told Logan, "but if she was walking with you right now, would that be a good thing?"

Logan smiled wide. He waggled his eyebrows. "It would be a very good thing."

I squeezed Emily's hand even harder.

Not that I was keeping score or anything—after all, this wasn't a basketball game, or even a Mathletes tournament— but Cupid Clara was one for one.

I was a matchmaking genius.

Chapter Ten

The opening day of the Austen Business Challenge was crazy busy. The seventh graders could arrive at school as early as 7:00 a.m. to set up their "storefronts," and they could open for business at 7:45 a.m. When Emily and I arrived at 7:15, more than half the tables in the front lobby of the school were already being set up.

Kacy's table was covered with a strip of Astroturf, and a soccer ball rested on an orange pylon next to a sign that read:

Kacy's Kicks

Take your soccer skills to the next level!
$5 for 30 minutes
$9 for 1 hour

"Your store looks awesome, Kace," I told her as Emily and I shuffled past awkwardly, carrying boxes and bags of all our stuff.

"Thanks!" she called after us. "I hope you guys will both sign up."

"After we get set up," I called back.

I looked around for the table with our names on it. We trudged past a dog walker, a temporary tattoo artist, a candy shop that made my mouth water, and a Go Green helper. Finally we found our table, at the far end of the lobby, right by the entrance to the main hallway of the school.

"Great location, right?" Alivia asked from the table right next to ours. She and Danielle were arranging dozens of cookies and mini muffins on different platters and tiered stands. She had all four of the cookies she had shown us last Monday at lunch, plus two kinds of muffins. "At first, Mr. Bersand had me all the way at the other end of the lobby by the trophy case. I mean, who ever goes by the trophy case? But I just told that kid in my Spanish class I needed to switch tables with his group."

I plunked my box down on the chair behind my table. "And they just switched with you? Didn't they want the good location?"

Alivia shrugged and straightened the thick black-and-white-striped cloth draped over her table. The front panel was embroidered with pink thread that spelled out *Sweet Alivia's*. On the corner of the table sat a stack of printed menus.

Both Danielle and Alivia wore black-and-white-striped aprons and had a pink cloth draped over each arm. They must have bought all their decorations. They looked pretty fancy. I wondered how Alivia had money for that in her budget. But I figured the pastry business must be a lot different from the matchmaking business.

Alivia waved her arm in the air as she answered me. "I don't think they even realized this was a good location. They were all too busy playing on their phones. They invented some dumb game. Their table didn't even have any decorations."

"That's so cool that they created their own game!" Emily set her box on the floor and opened it. She pulled out a plastic red-and-white polka-dot tablecloth and spread it over our table. "Do you know what the game is?"

Alivia rolled her eyes. "Do I look like I know? Or care?"

Emily and I raised our eyebrows at each other. Alivia was in a really bad mood about something.

"We'd better get our table set up," I said to Emily before Alivia's words had too much time to sting. I pulled out the wooden heart sign I'd collaged, and I set it above an arrow sign I'd made that read: THE CUPID IS IN. On the other side of the table, Emily set out a big bowl of Hershey's Kisses. Her idea was that chocolate would lure people to our table, and Kisses fit in with the Cupid theme.

I set out the tray of Cupid Clara questionnaires next to the bowl of Kisses, and then hung a little sign on the bowl: *Fill out a questionnaire and get two Kisses for* FREE. Even if all our questionnaires didn't turn into paying customers, they could still become someone else's potential match. We needed as many questionnaires as we could get.

Finally I pulled out my last decoration. It took me a long time to figure out how to make it, but I knew it was going to be worth it. Our "store" would really stand out. I bought a bunch of PVC pipe and connectors, the kind that plumbers use, and I painted them red. Emily and I assembled them together so they made a big square arch above our table.

Across the top of the arch I hung a banner I'd painted that read: *Find Your Match*. And dangling underneath it were cardboard cutout drawings of a mug of hot chocolate, a notebook and pencil, a video game controller, a dog, all the things people might have in common with their match. I also hung a bunch of Claragrams, with a scoreboard. It read: *Total Matches So Far: 1*. It was almost true. If anyone asked for the details, I'd just tell them the couple wasn't ready to go public yet.

When we finished, Emily and I walked to the opposite side of the lobby to check out our store. It definitely had the wow factor. I was going to be flooded with customers. Okay, okay, maybe I was getting ahead of myself. I still had a lot of work to do before that happened. Starting with client number one.

I nudged Emily with my elbow and leaned in close so I could speak in a low voice. "When should we tell Logan that you are his match?"

Emily shrugged, then pointed at our table. "Do you think we need a bigger sign for the Hershey's Kisses?"

"Stop changing the subject," I said. "He already knows anyway. And he told us he's super happy about it. The only thing left to do is make it official."

Emily shook her head and wrapped her arms around her body. "I know," she said, "but I just can't imagine actually saying it out loud. To his face. Every time I think about it, I get a huge stomachache. I'm not sure if *I* like him."

"Of course you like him." I patted Emily on the shoulder. She just needed some confidence. And once she was actually dating Logan, maybe she'd start to have some. "This sounds like the perfect time for another Claragram. I'll put one on his locker. This time it could say, *To meet your perfect match, go stand by the mural of the Austen Archer after school*. Then all you have to do is stand there. He'll know when he sees you. You won't have to say anything!"

Emily bit her lip and wrapped her arms tighter around her stomach. "Are you sure?"

I nodded, then grabbed her arm and led her back to our store. "Of course I'm sure. Trust me."

Even though it was a little before eight o'clock, the lobby was starting to fill up with students and teachers and even a few parents browsing all the tables. Alivia had a big crowd of kids standing around her table, and I could hear her taking order after order.

Emily and I took our seats behind the Cupid Clara table and waited. At first, a lot of kids walked by our table and looked at everything, but no one stopped to fill out a questionnaire.

"Maybe they're embarrassed?" Emily suggested.

I pressed a knuckle to my lips. I hadn't thought about that. I guess it *was* sort of embarrassing to fill out a questionnaire in front of a million people. I grabbed a piece of leftover poster board from one of the boxes I'd shoved under the table and quickly wrote a new sign in bubble letters.

Take One Questionnaire—Get a Kiss!
Fill It Out Later
Bring It Back—Get Another Kiss!

I put the sign behind the tray of questionnaires, just as a big group of sixth-grade girls approached our table.

"Take a chocolate and a questionnaire, you guys," I said. "You might find the perfect guy to dance with at the Hot Chocolate Social."

All the girls took one of each.

"Where do we put the questionnaires when we're done?" one of them asked.

I pointed to a red-and-white-striped box with a slit cut in the top. "In here," I told her. "Your questionnaire will be kept totally confidential and private. We are the only people who will ever see it."

The girls nodded and walked away.

After that, lots more people stopped by our table. They all took Kisses and questionnaires, but I lost count of how many we'd passed out because Alivia was talking at the top of her lungs and it was hard to tune her out. Either she was telling everyone to try her double chocolate mini muffins, or she was telling Danielle about how her father promised he'd take her to sample all the best pastry shops in Paris if she won the ABC.

I wondered if Alivia really had a shot at having the best business. Joey had said it was hard to have a business where you had to create new product every day. But at 8:15, when the first bell rang and we all started closing up our tables as the lobby cleared out, I heard Danielle say, "Can you believe it? We're sold out of everything! We made sixty dollars!"

"Shh!" said Alivia, keeping her voice low but loud enough so I could still hear it. "That's not a good thing, Danielle. We don't have anything to sell at lunch or after school."

"Oh," Danielle whispered loudly. "But still, sixty dollars is awesome!"

Sixty dollars? I looked at my completely empty cash box.

"Don't worry," Emily said. "Our business will just take a little longer to get going. Remember we don't make any money until you make matches. Once the questionnaires start coming back, Cupid Clara is going to take off!"

I nodded at Emily like I totally believed her, but my stomach writhed with doubt. What if no one returned a questionnaire? What if no one wanted a match? What if Cupid Clara set the record for the all-time worst business in Austen Middle School history?

Then I'd get a terrible report card, and Papi would send me away.

Chapter Eleven

The next morning, my dad woke me with the six most beautiful words in Spanglish. "Clara, it's a *día de nieve*."

"A snow day? For real?" I rolled over and rubbed my eyes sleepily. "Yay!" I cheered, my voice still soft and dreamy.

"I turned off your alarm," he whispered, tapping the clock on my nightstand. "You're welcome."

"Yeah, but you woke me anyway." I propped my arm up on one elbow. "Couldn't you have let me sleep in?"

"You did sleep in. It's already seven thirty. But I still have to go to work. I wanted to say good-bye before I left." He gave me two *besos* on my forehead. "Your mother called again," he said. "She said you didn't call her this week."

I pulled my comforter over my head. I usually talked to my mom every Sunday, but ever since Papi had told me she wanted me to come live with her, I'd been avoiding her calls.

He pulled the comforter back. "You need to call her today. Okay?"

I closed my eyes and curled into a ball. "Mmm-hmm," I said, even though I was really thinking about what else I could do today. It would be a good day to watch a couple of movies. Or maybe I'd text Alivia and see if anything was going on.

"Clara?" Papi said.

I opened one eye and looked at him.

"Is everything okay? At school? With your business? With . . ." He stared at the wall. "With everything?"

"Yeah, everything's great," I told him. So it was a little hard to keep up with my schoolwork and run a business. So I hadn't been able to officially make my first match yet. Papi didn't need to worry about those things. He didn't need to know about my problems.

"I have a bunch of stuff to work on today for my business," I added. Over twenty people had turned in questionnaires at lunchtime and after school, so I could finally make some good matches. I promised Kacy and Danielle they'd be next. "Can I invite some friends over when I'm done?"

Papi gave me a deep stare. "Boys?" he asked.

"Papi!" I wanted to crawl back down under the comforter. Why did he keep thinking I was looking for a boyfriend? I did not want to talk about that with him. "I was going to invite Emily and the girls."

Papi's face relaxed. "Okay, that's fine. But you'll have to shovel the sidewalk and the driveway when the snow stops. I don't want anyone slipping. Also, I asked Mrs. Kaufman to come check up on you in a few hours."

"I'm totally fine staying alone." I rolled my eyes, but Papi gave me a look. "Fine," I said, hugging Papi good-bye. Then I got out of bed and got dressed in my coziest leggings and sweatshirt.

Snow days were the best. For breakfast, I made myself a hot chocolate with cinnamon and chili powder, plus a tortilla with butter, sugar, and cinnamon. I watched the snow falling as I ate. The house was so quiet and still that it almost felt like I was the last person left on the earth.

is anything happening 2day? I texted Alivia. She didn't respond.

When I was finished eating, I got out the questionnaires and inputted all the answers in the special document Emily set up for me in Excel. I had forms from sixteen girls and six boys, which meant I needed to get more boys to fill out the questionnaire. But I was still able to make a bunch of matches. Kacy and Ryan were both soccer fanatics who liked watching superhero movies. Danielle and Connor both liked hanging out with friends, listening to dance music, and playing Monopoly. I had a feeling they'd be couples in no time.

what's up? I texted Emily. what are you doing 2day?

While I waited for her response, I pulled out my collage box and got to work on the Claragrams. I made one for Logan telling him it was time to meet his match, and I made a bunch more for my other couples telling them that I'd found their matches. When I was finished, I left them on the dining room table to dry and looked at the clock. It was only nine-thirty. I checked my phone. No one had texted me back yet. I sighed. This was going to be a long day.

I went into the living room to see if there were any good movies on TV, and finally, my phone buzzed. It was Emily.

stuck at home. my parents are at work.

me too, I replied.

Before I could text Emily more, I heard a scraping noise. I looked up and saw Joey, outside, shoveling our driveway. The snow hadn't stopped yet, but it was much lighter. It was probably smart to shovel now before the snow got any deeper. I put on my snow pants, boots, and coat and went into the garage to grab a shovel. After all, the driveway belonged to both of us, and it wasn't like I had anything else to do.

I pushed the button on the garage door opener, then stood behind the door, holding the shovel like a microphone, as the panels slowly raised in front of me like a curtain.

"Clara Martinez is in the house!" I said, striking a pose when the door was finally raised all the way. "I'm here to help!"

Joey's eyes scanned the driveway, which was about eighty percent cleared already. "Good timing," he said. "Arrive to help when the work's almost done."

"You should have called me," I said, stepping out into the snow. "I didn't even realize you were out here until a few minutes ago."

Joey shrugged. "You were busy doing your art. I didn't want to interrupt you. You looked so focused."

"How did you— you were peeking through my windows! Joey!" I raised my shovel in front of me like a sword. "I can't believe you were spying on me!"

Joey shook his head, and I thought his cheeks looked a little redder, though they were already pretty red from the cold and the shoveling. "I wasn't peeking in your windows. I went to ring your doorbell, and I saw you through the front." He pointed at the bay window next to the porch. It gave a perfect view of the dining room table.

"Oh," I said, lowering my shovel. I climbed up onto my front stoop and started shoveling off the top. "Well, thanks, then. I was working on Cupid Clara stuff."

Joey got back to work on the driveway, his shovel making rhythmic scrapes against the asphalt as he cleared shovelful after shovelful easily. My own shovel kept catching on chunks of ice, or maybe I just didn't know how to do it as well as Joey because my shovel scrapes sounded ragged and uneven.

"So how's your business going?" he asked, tossing some snow on my front lawn.

I tried to toss my shovelful of snow on the lawn as well, but most of it landed on the bottom two steps of the porch. I'd have to shovel it all again when I got down there. "Pretty good," I told him. "My first couple is almost official, and I made a bunch of new matches today."

"Who's your first couple?" he asked.

I arched an eyebrow at him. "I can't tell you that. It's confidential. But I have a feeling you'll find out soon. I don't think the guy will wait until the Hot Chocolate Social. I think he's going to ask Em—I mean, I think he's going to ask *the girl* to go out with him. Like, officially."

"Wait a minute." Joey stopped working and rested his elbow on the handle of his shovel. "Please tell me your first couple is not Emily and Logan."

My breath caught a little bit, but I kept shoveling and acted like his words meant nothing to me. "I told you. It's confidential. I can't say." I cleared the last bit of snow from the top of the porch and started on the first step. "Why?"

"It is them, isn't it?" Joey pushed his shovel through the last strip of snow on the driveway, then started shoveling my sidewalk.

I kept my lips pressed tightly together, mostly because I didn't want to say anything, but a little because I was starting to be annoyed. What did Joey know about fixing people up?

"I don't think she's the kind of girl he would go for," Joey said.

"You don't even know him! Or her. How can you say that?" I was surprised Joey would judge someone from seeing them for only a few seconds.

"I see him and his basketball friends in the hallways after math tournaments. He's loud. It's not hard to get a sense of what he's like."

My breathing was starting to speed up, and it wasn't just because shoveling was hard work. I felt like I wanted to dump a shovelful of snow all over Joey's head. Instead I tossed it toward my yard. It landed on the bottom step again and made me even madder. "For your information, I happen to know he *does* like Emily."

"He told you that?" Joey reached the end of my sidewalk and started on the bottom step of my porch. I moved down to the second step and took a deep breath, trying to calm myself.

"Yeah," I said. "He did."

Joey pursed his mouth in disbelief, but he said, "Wow, okay. I guess I was wrong."

"You'd think by now you'd be used to the feeling," I said, trying for a joke. It didn't come out funny. I took a deep breath. I hated fighting with Joey. It just got me so angry when he acted like he knew everything. Joey didn't say anything, so I made the joke again. "You know, since you're nearly always wrong, and I'm nearly always right."

I finished clearing the second step and stepped down to the third. With Joey one step below me, our eyes were practically at the same height.

"Ha-ha," Joey said, looking straight at me. His eyelashes looked long and feathery, and there was one snowflake perched on the end of his right lash. I wanted to reach out and brush it away, but for some reason, my arms wouldn't move. I just stood there looking at Joey as he stood there looking at me. Then I got the weirdest feeling in my body, like the snow was falling inside me, but I wasn't cold. I felt warm.

Finally I got de-hypnotized. I shook my head and took a step backward.

"You have snow on your eyelash," I said.

Joey wiped the wrong eye, gripped his shovel again, and started clearing the rest of the bottom step. "What are you doing today?" he asked, nudging me up a step so he could finish the one I was standing on too.

"I don't know," I said. When I was little, my mother used to make snow days feel like a big party. We'd bake something really complicated like *tres leches* or *sopapillas*, and we'd be so covered in flour we'd look like the snowy evergreen trees in our front yard. Then we'd eat dessert for lunch, blast her favorite music, and dance around the house.

I sighed. "I'll probably sit around bored out of my mind."

"Want to watch a movie?" Joey asked. "My sister invited about eighty-four of her closest friends over, and if I stay at home, I'll have to hide in my room all day."

"Sure," I said, trying not to smile too much. Seriously, I reminded myself. It was just Joey. I hung out with him all the time. I paused at the doorway for a second, remembering Papi's question about having boys over, but he meant *real* boys, boys that might try to be my secret admirer kind of boys. He couldn't have meant Joey. I opened the door and gestured for Joey to enter.

Inside, I made us more hot chocolate while Joey looked over my shoulder.

"Hey, you want to try my special hot chocolate recipe?" Joey asked, turning around to rummage through my cabinets before I could even answer. He had been to my house so many times that he knew his way around our kitchen.

Wordlessly, I watched as Joey grabbed a jar of peanut butter and a spoon, and scooped a small dollop into my cup of hot chocolate, stirring gently. He then did the same for his cup.

"Trust me," he said, handing me my steaming mug.

I was used to hot chocolate only one way—with cinnamon and chili powder—so I was very skeptical. I took a sip anyway and was pleasantly surprised. "Yum!"

Joey laughed. "See? Chocolate and peanut butter are great together."

I thought about what he said for a second. Where had I heard something like that before? But before I could figure it out, Joey was already heading toward the living room, so I quickly followed him.

"*The Avengers*? *Star Wars*? *Chicken Little*?" Joey scrolled through the movie guide, offering suggestions.

Finally, when we couldn't agree on anything else, we chose *Finding Nemo*. It had been our favorite when we were little. I brought out both our drinks and settled into the couch on the opposite end from Joey.

We were just about to start the movie, when my doorbell rang.

I jumped, then laughed. I was really glad Joey was here, because I wasn't expecting anyone, and if the doorbell rang unexpectedly when I was alone, I'd instantly be certain that it was a kidnapper. Even with Joey in my house, I was half sure there was a burglar at my door.

"I don't think we should answer it," I said.

"Okay." Joey shrugged. "It's probably some delivery guy. Want me to check?"

I shook my head no, and grabbed a blanket and pulled it up to my chin. The doorbell rang again. Joey stood up and walked to the corner of the room where he could look through the bay window and see the front porch.

"It's some guy from your grade," he said. "From school."

I let the blanket drop. "Who? Logan?" Maybe he couldn't wait to find out that Emily was his match!

Joey shook his head. "I don't remember his name, but he's just as bad as Logan."

I rolled my eyes at him as I got up to answer the door. I was pretty sure that no one in my grade was a kidnapper or a burglar, so I wasn't too worried anymore.

"Mateo?" I said when I saw him standing on my front porch holding an empty blue-and-white casserole dish. "What are you doing here?"

He leaned backward and studied the address numbers next to the porch light. "Isn't this Sofia's house?"

"*Sofia's* house?" I wrinkled my face in confusion. My heart sped up and my muscles tensed, like they wanted to run away and hide. I looked behind him to see if I could see any of the other guys from school. Maybe this was some kind of prank.

He held up the casserole dish. "My mom wanted me to

return this. She and Sofia's mom are friends. I thought this was the address she told me."

"One of you must have gotten the numbers mixed up. She's 878; we're 887."

"Oh." Mateo nodded his head at my explanation. Behind him, the snow started falling heavier. The snowflakes looked like pillow feathers.

"Your mom made you go out in a snowstorm to return a dish?" I shook my head and widened my eyes in disbelief. "That's rough."

"Oh, yeah. She's, um, she can be tough." Mateo stammered and looked at his boots as he spoke. "Maybe, um, since I'm here . . . now would be a good time for me to ask you that question."

A gust of wind blew a puff of snow into my house. The snowstorm had picked up even more. "Joey! Look at the driveway. We're going to have to do it all over again."

Joey walked over to the window, then folded his arms over his chest and peered down his nose at me. "We? I don't remember you doing much driveway shoveling."

The wind blew another burst of snow through the door. The icy flakes stung my face.

"Ay!" I shouted. "Mateo, come in before we freeze to death!"

Mateo came inside, closed the door, and stomped the snow off his boots.

"Don't you live over by the fire station? It must have taken you forever to walk here!" I shook my head. He lived at least two miles from me.

"Why wouldn't your mom just drive you?" Joey asked.

Mateo laughed. He sounded nervous. Maybe it was just the cold. "I was bored, I guess. Walking here seemed like a good idea at the time."

I looked out the window, and all I could see was a swirling mess of white. "I don't think you can walk home for a while now. It's crazy out there," I told him.

Mateo looked out the window longingly. He probably had plans with the basketball guys or something. Then he looked back at me, and a sheepish smile spread across his face. He glanced over at Joey. "Sorry. I didn't realize you had company."

"Oh, that's okay," I said, giving Joey an "I'm sorry" look over Mateo's shoulder. Joey rolled his eyes. "We were just going to watch *Finding Nemo*," I told him. "Did you still want to ask me that question?"

"What?" Mateo shook his head. "Oh, yeah." He looked at Joey again. "No, that's okay. I'll ask you some other time."

Mateo plunked himself down on the couch right between my spot and Joey's spot. He picked up Joey's hot chocolate and took a sip. "This is great. You got any popcorn?"

I wondered what my dad would say about having two boys in my house today. Maybe I could convince Alivia and everyone to come over too. I picked up my phone to text her and realized Emily had been trying to get a hold of me all morning.

> kacy said alivia is having everyone over. kacy's mom is driving. want a ride?
>
> txt me back soon if u want a ride.
>
> srsly, kacy's mom wants to go before snow gets worse.
>
> r u there?
>
> srry. we can't wait anymore. txt me that u r ok, plz!
>
> ugh. we r planning alivia's outfits for this week. wish u were here.

I quickly texted Emily back.

> sorry was shoveling driveway.

I thought about telling her what was happening at my house today, but decided against it.

> am fine. have fun. talk 2nite?

I went into the kitchen and tossed a bag of popcorn into the microwave, and when I came back with three bowls, I had to blink a couple of times at the picture of Joey and Mateo sitting on my couch together.

Mateo was telling Joey all about the special hair gel he uses, and Joey was staring at the ceiling like he hoped a giant claw would lower down and lift him away. I felt bad for him, but it was also kind of funny. I wasn't even sure if Joey knew what hair gel was.

This day certainly wasn't going the way I'd imagined it, but maybe something good could come out of it too. I still needed more guys to fill out my questionnaires.

"Hey, Mateo," I said, handing him a bowl of popcorn, "you know my business, Cupid Clara?"

He shoved a handful of popcorn into his mouth and nodded as popcorn crumbs spilled all down his shirt.

"Do you think you could get your friends to stop by my table? They don't even have to buy anything, just fill out my form. And they'll get free chocolate."

"Sure," he said as he ate another giant handful of popcorn. "I'll make everyone do it tomorrow."

I leaned back into the couch and pushed PLAY on the remote. The movie started as a big gust of wind rattled the front window of my house. I pulled my knees to my chest and wrapped my blanket tighter around me.

Then the doorbell rang again. My heart started. Who could it be this time? I paused the movie and gave Joey a look so he'd know to walk with me to the door in case of burglars.

It wasn't a burglar. It was Mrs. Kaufman, the old lady who lived down the street. I'd forgotten Papi had told her to check on me. She wore a clear plastic hat over her curly gray hair, and a puffy down coat that went all the way to her feet.

"Hi, sweetie," she said. "Are you doing okay? Do you need anything?"

"I'm fine, Mrs. Kaufman. Thank you."

"Hello, Joseph," she said, nodding at Joey. Then peering over my shoulder, I saw her notice Mateo.

"Uh, my dad said I could have friends over," I explained, the tips of my ears burning.

She nodded, and stepped inside. "Yes, he did say you

might have friends here. I'll stay out of your way. Don't worry. I brought a book and I remember where you keep your tea."

Mrs. Kaufman hung her coat in the closet, then introduced herself to Mateo before heading to the kitchen. Joey and I settled back on the couch, and I turned the movie on again. The sounds of Mrs. Kaufman searching through our cupboards mixed with the sounds of the movie. Mateo shoveled handful after handful of popcorn into his mouth.

I leaned backward a little bit so I could see Joey's face on the other side of Mateo. Just as I did, Joey looked over at me and smiled, and my whole body started sweating like we were in the middle of a tropical heat wave instead of a blizzard. I quickly looked back at the TV, and I hoped I wasn't getting sick or anything.

Chapter Twelve

The next morning, Papi drove me to school. It took forever to get there because we had to drive all around the outside of town. A big water pipe had burst near the downtown area, and police were redirecting traffic. That meant I had an extra long time of Papi asking me questions.

"So, how did your call with Mami go?" He kept his eyes on the road while he spoke, which was good. If he looked at my face, I'd have to tell him the truth, and right now it didn't feel like an option.

"I forgot to call her," I lied. "I got busy with stuff yesterday."

Papi frowned. "You have to call her, *mija.*"

"*Lo sé*. I know." I leaned my head all the way back against the headrest.

"What kept you so busy yesterday?"

"Well, shoveling the driveway, working on Cupid Clara." Watching movies with Joey and Mateo, but Papi didn't need a reminder about that.

He tapped his fingers on the steering wheel as he drove. "Did the rest of your friends ever come over?" he asked. "Mrs. Kaufman only told me about two of them."

I hugged my backpack to my chest and shook my head. "No," I replied just as we pulled up to the school. Whew. "Thanks for the ride," I told my father. "See you tonight."

I closed the door before he could ask me anything else. I was crazy late. I hoped Emily was on time; otherwise no one would be running our table and our customers wouldn't be able to pick up or drop off their questionnaires.

I rushed over to the Cupid Clara table, but stopped dead in my tracks when I saw Emily sitting at the table. She looked *so* sad. I pushed past the guy taking a questionnaire and gave Emily a big hug.

"Are you all right?" I whispered in her ear.

Emily gave a big fake laugh. "I'm fine. Evan was just

picking up a questionnaire." I turned around and realized Evan Cho was the person standing at our table.

"Make sure to tell all your friends to fill them out too," I told him. I'm sure there were plenty of girl math geeks I could match him with.

Evan nodded at Emily, nodded at me, then walked away.

"What was that about?" I asked.

Emily swallowed. "He wanted to let me know that he was going to be karate sparring partners with Rajiv from now on. I have to find a new partner."

"Oh," I said. "But that won't be hard, will it? Can't your sensei help you find one?"

"Yeah," said Emily, her voice was flat.

I needed to cheer her up ASAP. No one would want to sign up with a mopey matchmaker.

I picked up the questionnaire box and shook it. I heard a bunch of papers rattling around inside, but I knew we could do even better. "Want to make a scene? Get everyone even more excited about Cupid Clara?"

Emily sighed and shrugged. This wasn't like her at all. I had to act fast. I looked at the bowl of chocolate. "I've got an idea," I told her. "Do we have more bags of Kisses?"

Emily looked in the box underneath the table. "Four more," she said.

"Okay, here goes nothing." I picked up the bowl of Kisses and stood on top of my chair. Then I took a deep breath and shouted at the top of my lungs. "Anyone who fills out a Cupid Clara questionnaire in the next fifteen minutes gets a whole handful of Hershey's Kisses! As many as they can grab without spilling!"

For a second, the whole room paused and everyone just stared at me like I was crazy. I had bad memory of second grade, the week after my mom left and my dad made me go back to school and I got out at hopscotch and couldn't stop crying. Everyone had stared at me then too.

But a second later, nearly half the people in the lobby flooded our table. Emily and I started handing out blank questionnaires and pens, and I reminded everyone that they didn't get their Kisses until they put their finished questionnaires in the box.

"I'm not sure *bribing* customers is a good business strategy," Alivia called to me from her table, laughing. "You're going to spend more money than you earn."

I laughed too. "It's not bribery," I told her. "We're incentivizing." The chocolates were in our budget, and they were working. Our table was flooded with customers.

I noticed Alivia's table was down to one tray of cookies left. "Wow, you've nearly sold out again!" I said. "Awesome!"

Alivia gave me a funny look, and I remembered that she didn't want to sell out so early in the day. Now she'd have nothing left to sell at lunch.

"Maybe you could raise your prices?" I suggested. "Then you'd make more money even if you can't make more treats."

Alivia wrinkled her nose. "There are two other groups selling baked goods," she told me. "If we raise our prices, everyone will just start buying more from them." She sighed, turning away from me.

I wished I had some advice for her, but I didn't, so I asked Emily if she could handle the store for the last five minutes until the bell rang. "I want to deliver our Claragrams," I told her.

"Sure," Emily said. "No problem."

"By the way." I held up Logan's Claragram. "You need to be standing by the Austen Archer after school."

Emily's eyes widened in terror, but I raced away before she could argue. This was going to be just the thing to cheer her up *and* to turn all those new questionnaires into matches.

I speed-walked to the language arts hallway, since that's where most of the sixth-grade lockers were, and taped my perfect-match announcements on my newest couples' lockers. Then I taped Danielle's, Kacy's, Connor's, and Ryan's hearts on *their* lockers. Finally, I raced to Logan's locker. I only had one minute left until the first bell would ring, and the hallway would start filling up. I wanted to do it before I was surrounded by a million people.

I tore off a piece of tape and pressed the glittery heart to the locker.

"What's that?"

Logan's voice made me jump.

"You weren't supposed to see me doing this!" I said as Logan peered at the Claragram on his locker.

"Why should we wait until after school?" he asked. "You're already here."

I wagged my finger at him. "Just think of how exciting it will be when you walk to the archer and see your match."

"I can see her right now," Logan said.

I looked over my shoulder, panicked, because if Emily was in the hallway, then something bad must have happened at our table. But no one was in the hallway. It was empty. I looked back at Logan, my eyebrows squeezing in confusion.

He was looking at my chin. "Clara," he said. "Will you go out with me?"

"What?" What was Logan saying? Did he want me to walk him to the archer? Was he nervous about seeing Emily alone? Maybe they really were just like each other.

"I don't want to wait until after school to ask you," he said. "I *like* you. Will you go out with me?"

I blinked a bunch of times. "You like *me*?"

He punched me on the shoulder. "Duh!"

My ears were hearing Logan's words, but my brain did not understand. How could he like me? He practically told me he liked Emily the other day at the basketball game. "Don't you mean Emily? You like Emily. I know you do. *She's* your match. Are you saying you want me to ask her for you?"

Logan wrinkled his nose. "*Emily?* Uh-uh. She's nice, I guess, but she's a little boring."

I opened my mouth to say something else, but all my words disappeared. I just stood and stared at him open-mouthed like a dead fish.

"So, do you want to go out or not?" Logan asked me again.

Finally my words came back to me.

"N-no," I stammered. Then I tried to be a little nicer. "Sorry."

"*No?*" He looked at me wide-eyed, like he couldn't believe what he was hearing.

"I like you as a friend," I explained. "I could never think of you as more than that. I'm not interested in going out with anyone." I shook my head back and forth really fast to help make my point.

"But you totally made it seem like you liked me," he said. "You did like me. I know it." Logan was staring at me and shaking his head, like he thought I was speaking gibberish.

I wanted to shake him, make him understand. It was a simple mistake. "This was just a mix-up. I honestly thought you liked Emily."

"And *I* thought *you* liked me. I *saw* you putting notes on my locker."

"That was for Emily!" I threw my hands up into the air. This was a disaster. No one would trust my matchmaking business if they found out about this. And Emily. Would she hate me for convincing her to like Logan? And if Emily hated me, how would Alivia feel? Would she let me hang out with her anymore?

The bell rang, and students started filing into the hallway, opening their lockers and crowding around me and Logan.

"I *know* you liked me!" Logan grabbed the Claragram and crumpled it in his fist, then he dropped it on the floor at my feet and stormed off, leaving me to clean up the glittery mess.

I spent the rest of the day avoiding Emily, Alivia, and everyone I could. I didn't even help with Cupid Clara at lunchtime. I told Emily I had to catch up on homework, but instead I hid in the bathroom. Just like Old Clara used to do when Sofia was home sick.

When the final bell rang, I couldn't put it off any longer. After school, I met Emily by the mural of the Austen Archer.

"I'm so sorry!" I said when I was standing close enough

that no one would overhear. "There was a big misunder-standing." I explained how Logan thought the notes were from me, so that's who he decided to like. "Please don't be mad at me," I said. "I'll find you an even better match. I promise."

"It's okay." Emily hugged me and then gave me a sweet dimply smile. "Of course he liked you. Who wouldn't like you? I bet every guy in the school likes you."

"Now you're being crazy," I said, shaking my head at her, but feeling my chest expanding with relief. I was so glad Emily didn't hate me for my mistake. "Anyway, I'm not interested in finding a guy for myself."

"Really?" Emily and I walked down the hall and out the door in the cold wintery afternoon. "You don't like *any-one*?" she asked just before we each headed our separate ways home.

"Nope." I shook my head. "I don't really believe in that kind of stuff."

Emily blinked her eyes in confusion, like she didn't understand what I meant.

"It's no big deal," I told her. "I prefer making the matches anyway."

As I walked to my house, I thought about the red folder filled with new questionnaires in my backpack. Even though Mateo hadn't come through on his promise to get his friends to fill out the questionnaires, I still had about forty new forms to go through over the weekend. I would get to make a lot of matches.

Hopefully Logan would forget about my goof by Monday. It's not as if he'd want to tell everyone the whole story either. He was probably almost as embarrassed as I was. Cupid Clara had about a dozen other matches in the works already. As long as Logan didn't tell anyone about my matchmaking mix-up, Cupid Clara would be fine.

Chapter Thirteen

On Saturday night, Emily came to my house for a sleep-over. Alivia was having another one of her boy-girl parties, but I told her I had a family thing to do and Emily told her she didn't feel well. Normally I would have thought it was a terrible idea to miss one of Alivia's parties, but Alivia had been acting a little out of sorts lately and Logan was going to be there. I didn't want to face him so soon after my mistake.

Papi let Emily and me order pizza, and he went into his office, so we had the whole living room to ourselves.

"Okay," I said, pulling out the big box of Cupid Clara questionnaires, "let's see if there is someone better in there for you."

I never should have matched Logan and Emily. I'd known they weren't right for each other, and I should have trusted my gut. I blushed when I remembered Joey had been right about Logan. I hadn't wanted to listen.

Emily took a bite of pizza and let the gooey cheese stretch for a while before she snapped it off. "I don't know," she said when she finished chewing. "Let's just make the best matches we can. If we don't find someone for me, I'll be okay. Maybe I'll follow your lead and decide not to like anyone at all."

I studied Emily's face to see if she really meant it. There wasn't anything wrong with not liking anyone, of course. But Emily *wanted* to like someone. I could tell. Still, I didn't want to get her hopes up for nothing. This time I wasn't going to encourage her until I'd found her the perfect match.

"Okay," I said, dumping all the questionnaires out on the dining room table. "Let's get matching."

Emily and I started sorting through each of the questionnaires one by one. Emily would read me the answers, and I would input the data onto a spreadsheet on my computer. That made it easier to see all the people who had similar answers. I noticed lots of potential couples as we went along, but I wanted to wait until all the questionnaires were recorded before we started making any official matches.

"Okay, who's next?" I asked Emily, clicking on a new field on my spreadsheet.

Emily picked up the next questionnaire from the pile, unfolded it, then said, "Oh my gosh." She put both hands over her mouth and shook her head. "This is so sweet."

"What?" I asked, leaning closer to peer over her shoulder. She held the paper out of sight.

"I don't know if you're going to like it," she said.

"What is it?" I asked, starting to get exasperated.

"Just remember it's sweet. And it's fun." Emily handed me the paper. It was a Cupid Clara questionnaire. Then I looked more closely.

CUPID CLARA QUESTIONNAIRE

Name: I LIKE TO THINK OF MYSELF AS CLARA'S PERFECT MATCH.

Age: MENTAL AGE OR BIOLOGICAL AGE?

Birthday: NO THANK YOU, I ALREADY HAVE ONE.

Favorites

Subject in school: I LIKE ANY SUBJECT WHEN IT'S INTERESTING AND NO SUBJECTS WHEN THEY ARE BORING.

After-school activity: AFTER I'M DONE WITH SCHOOL, I'LL PROBABLY GET A JOB, NOT AN ACTIVITY, BUT "AFTER SCHOOL" WON'T BE FOR A WHILE SINCE I PLAN TO GO TO COLLEGE AND THEN MAYBE MEDICAL SCHOOL.

Hobbies: YES, I HAVE A LOT OF THEM. REALLY, REALLY INTERESTING ONES. BUT IF I TOLD YOU, YOU MIGHT REALIZE WHO I AM.

Animal: WHALES. DID YOU KNOW THAT COMPARED TO HUMANS WHALE IQs ARE ABOUT 2,000?

Food: MEXICAN, ITALIAN, JAPANESE, INDIAN, FRENCH, AND AMERICAN

Dessert: REESE'S PEANUT BUTTER CUPS

Type of music: JAZZ

Which do you prefer . . .

Watching movies or TV shows?: YES

Board games or video games?: BORED GAMES

Being inside or outside?: WHEN I'M INSIDE, I WANT TO BE OUTSIDE, AND WHEN I'M OUTSIDE, I WANT TO BE INSIDE. AND VICE VERSA. OR, WHEREVER CLARA IS.

Random Questions

What are three words you'd pick to describe yourself?: SMART, FUNNY, COOL, GOOD-LOOKING, INNUMERATE

Is the glass half-empty or half-full?: YOU ARE MISSING THE POINT. THE GLASS IS REFILLABLE.

Why did you cross the road?: TO TURN IN MY QUESTIONNAIRE.

When I finally put the questionnaire down, Emily was staring at me with a dreamy expression in her eyes. "That was awesome!" she said. "I wish a guy would write that for me."

Aha! I knew she was lying about not wanting a boyfriend. But that was beside the point. "I guess it was pretty cute, but I'm still not interested," I said, even though my heart was pounding.

"How can you say that? You don't even know who wrote it!" She threw her hands up in the air. "Wait a minute. *Do* you know who wrote it?"

I shook my head. "But this isn't the first note I've gotten. I—I think I have a secret admirer." I blushed and told Emily all about the note in my locker and the smushed package of peanut butter cups.

"You are so lucky!" she squealed. "We have to try to figure out who it is."

I folded the paper back up and tossed it to the other side of the table. "We definitely don't have to figure out who wrote it. What we have to do is finish making all our matches." I pointed at the stack of papers in front of Emily. "Let's get back to work."

She made a little saluting motion with her hand. Then she smacked her palm on her forehead. "Wait. What if it was from Logan? What if he still wants to go out with you, and he's trying to prove to you that you guys would be a great match?"

"It's not Logan," I said, pointing at the papers again. "Work."

"But how do you know?" she asked. "It could definitely be from Logan. Do you still have his other questionnaire so we could compare the handwriting?"

I sighed when I remembered that I'd actually given him two questionnaires, so I started digging through my folder for Logan's real questionnaire. Emily went to the other side of the table and grabbed the secret admirer paper. When we put them side by side, the results were inconclusive. Whoever the secret admirer was, he'd written super neatly. It was impossible to tell if the same person had written both.

Seeing Logan's questionnaire again, though, I was reminded that his favorite dessert was Reese's Peanut Butter Cups. Which was what my secret admirer put on his questionnaire—and what he had left for me in my locker.

"Don't those *P*s look the same? I really think this could be from Logan," Emily said.

"It's not from Logan because I don't want it to be from Logan!" I finally said, my voice rising a little louder than I'd intended it to.

"What's not from Logan?" Papi asked. I spun around and saw him standing in the kitchen making himself a cup of coffee. My palms began to sweat. How long had he been listening. "Who's Logan?"

Emily put her hand over her mouth to hide her giggles. But to me, this was no laughing matter. "Logan is some kid who goes to our school, Papi. You don't know him."

Papi dropped a cinnamon stick into his mug. "So what did he give you?"

"Nothing! We were just trying to figure out who wrote this one questionnaire," I told him. "The writing's really messy."

Papi looked at me like he didn't believe me. Then he said, "Mami called me again. She's waiting."

My eyes darted to Emily. She knew my parents were divorced, but she didn't know the whole story of how my mother had left me with Papi so she could figure out her life.

"Can we talk about this later?" I said through clenched teeth.

"Okay. Good night." Papi blew on his coffee and took a sip. "In bed by eleven."

"I know," I said.

"Good night, Mr. Martinez," Emily called out.

When my dad was gone, Emily and I turned back to each other awkwardly.

"Your dad is so young," she said. "He looks like a movie star."

"He and my mom got married when he was twenty-two," I told her. "It was right after Papi graduated from college. She was only twenty. They had me a year later."

"I don't think I've ever seen your mom around," she said softly.

"She lives in Texas," I told her, then suddenly I wanted to tell her everything. Or at least part of everything. "That's where her family's from. She moved back there when I was eight so that she could go to college. Now she's a nurse."

"Whoa." Emily blinked a couple times. "I can't imagine living so far away from my mom. Do you miss her?"

I shook my head. "I talk to her every week and visit her for a month in the summer." When she'd first left to go live near her mother and brothers and sisters, she'd been very unhappy, she told me. She was trying to figure out who she was and what she wanted to do. For some reason, that meant she couldn't talk to me or Papi at all. For one whole year. Then she went back to school, and she called us up and said she wanted to be part of our lives again. By then, I was used to living without her. She was my mother, but no matter what Papi called her, she'd never be my *mami* again.

Chapter Fourteen

Monday morning, I arrived at school early, ready to put the whole Logan mix-up behind me. From all the new questionnaires I'd collected on Friday, I had eighteen Claragrams to pass out. Even without my original couple of Emily and Logan, lots of people were interested in finding their matches.

I headed over to my table, and changed the sign so it read TOTAL MATCHES SO FAR: 34.

I couldn't wait to see how many more people had signed up. Then I stopped short.

Logan was standing next to our table. For a second, I thought maybe he'd decided that he *did* like Emily after all.

But when I got a little closer, I could see that Emily had her nose buried in her phone, and Logan was actually standing at Alivia and Danielle's table. My stomach wobbled nervously. But maybe he was just there for the mini muffins.

"Hey, Em. What's up?" I said, plunking my backpack down next to my chair and pointing my eyebrows toward Logan.

Emily didn't look up from her phone, so she didn't realize what I was actually asking.

"I bought that game those kids who used to sit next to us made," Emily told me. "It's called Hoppy Frog, and I can't stop playing it!"

"Cool," I said, looking at her screen over her shoulder. A little green frog was hopping across a pond catching flies. Then it missed a lily pad and fell in the water. Game over.

"We made so many matches this weekend!" I told her. I spread all my Claragrams on the table in front of me. "Look what I did yesterday!"

"That's awesome," Emily said, beaming.

"I guess *some* people need help finding someone to like," I heard Logan say behind me. His voice was loud enough for me to hear it, and I was pretty sure that was on purpose. He obviously wasn't going to let me forget my tiny mistake.

"Not us," Alivia said.

Us? Alivia liked *Logan?* Was he the boy she'd been crushing on? No wonder she'd been upset. I wanted to turn my head and look, but I didn't want to seem like I was eavesdropping. I looked at Emily instead. Her whole face was pinker than cotton candy, but she kept her eyes focused on her game.

"Luckily I don't need a Cupid," Logan added. "I like a girl who just comes up to you and asks you to go out." I heard a shuffling noise, and then Logan said in a much quieter voice, "Ow! What was that for?"

Alivia whispered something back at him, but she clearly didn't want me to hear because her voice was way too quiet.

I was happy for them, but I didn't want Emily to feel bad. I scooped all the Claragrams into a pile and handed them to Emily. "I'll watch the store today. Why don't you go pass these out? Here's the list of locker numbers."

Emily took the Claragrams and walked off holding them in one hand and playing Hoppy Frog with the other. She almost ran smack into Mateo. He saw her coming, though, and did a funny twirl spin to avoid her. Then he darted back over to Cupid Clara and rested both hands on the table.

"Finally here to sign up?" I asked him. "I thought you were going to bring all your friends."

"What?" Mateo looked confused at first, then he remembered. "Oh, sorry. I forgot. I'll do that later." He looked both ways, then leaned closer and lowered his voice. "Did you hear about Holy Cross?"

I could practically feel Alivia leaning closer too, to try to hear what Mateo was saying.

I shook my head. "What about it?"

"Their whole school was flooded when that pipe burst last week. They're trying to fix it now, and all the kids get to stay home from school this week. But if they can't fix it after that, they might send the kids here until the school is fixed."

My head went fuzzy at Mateo's words. I felt like I had seashells pressed up against either ear, the sound of my blood whooshing around my head growing louder and louder as my heart beat faster and faster. The kids from Holy Cross? Coming to my new school?

"All of them?" I asked. My voice came out strangely high and squeaky.

Mateo shook his head. "Some of them would go to St. Norbert's, but it's kind of far, so some of them would come here. But only if they can't fix the school."

Please not Sofia, I thought. *Please let Sofia go to St. Norbert's.*

"Do you think Sofia would come here?" he whispered.

My eyes flew up to his. Why would he ask me that? Sometimes it seemed like Mateo wanted to be my friend, but sometimes it seemed like he wanted to torment me.

"What are you guys talking about?" Alivia called from her table.

"Nothing," Mateo and I both said at the same time.

Weird. If Mateo wanted to tease me, he sure didn't want anyone else to know about it.

"Are you guys talking about Holy Cross?" Alivia straightened her platter of mini cinnamon rolls. I noticed she seemed to have a lot more treats today. Her tabletop was full, and under the table were several more boxes filled with cookies and brownies. "When I was on a cruise over break, I met a guy who goes there," Alivia told us. "His name is T. J., do you know him?"

My heart started pounding. Had T. J. told Alivia about me?

"Everybody knows everybody at Holy Cross," Mateo said. "It's a small school."

This conversation was starting to get dangerously close to my past.

"Sorry," I said to Mateo, "but I need to get back to work. Nobody's turned in a questionnaire or requested my matchmaking help this whole morning. I think they think I'm busy or something."

Mateo looked surprised that I was asking him to leave. But did he really think I'd want to reminisce about the bad old days?

"I still *really* need your advice," he whispered.

"Sure, anytime." I was starting to think this whole secret-advice thing was just a crazy game Mateo was playing with my mind or something.

But he gave me his huge, sparkly smile. "Thanks!" he called as he jogged off.

"No problem," I said, grabbing a bag of Hershey's Kisses from under the table and refilling the bowl. "Do you guys want some free chocolate?" I asked a group of eighth-grade boys from the debate team. "All you have to do is fill out a questionnaire."

They looked up at my sign, and then at each other. "No thanks," one of them said. Then they headed over to Alivia's table and bought a dozen mini cinnamon rolls.

"Hey, there!" I beckoned to a group of girls I knew from my Skills for Life class. "Do you guys want to find out who your perfect match is?"

As soon as the words left my mouth, the girls scattered around the lobby, avoiding my table like the plague. I didn't understand. Last week, Cupid Clara had been one of the most popular businesses in the school. Today, I could barely get a customer to look at me.

Alivia kicked Danielle under the table. Danielle gave her a look and held up one finger. Alivia kicked her again.

"Clara," Danielle said to me, "what's up with your business today? It seems like no one wants you to make them a match anymore."

Danielle was asking me a question, but her voice sounded

flat. Like she wasn't really looking for an answer. And Alivia was busy selling someone a blueberry scone, but I could tell that she was listening to us. A little smile tugged at her lips.

"I don't know." I tried to act as casual as possible, but inside I was worried. "I'm sure it's no big deal. Maybe people don't like thinking about matches first thing on a Monday morning."

"Maybe." Alivia handed Logan a scone and adjusted the giant stack of silver bracelets on her arm. "Do you think people are worried about the quality of your matches?"

I looked back and forth between Alivia and Logan, wondering what she was really trying to tell me. Logan had obviously told her about my mix-up. But how many other people had he told?

I shrugged. "Nobody's perfect." I picked up the pile of questionnaires and tapped the edges of the paper on the table to make them even. "But I've still made lots of good matches. Hey, Danielle, I have a great idea. Why don't you let me connect you and your match? I'll do it for free. It can be part of my advertising budget. I just need to you tell everyone how happy you are if it works out."

"That would be awesome!" Danielle exclaimed. Alivia kicked her again. "Sorry!" Danielle told her. "But every time I try to talk to him, my mouth gets all dry and my lips start sticking to my teeth. I look like I'm wearing dentures. How am I supposed to tell him I like him if I look like I'm wearing dentures?"

"Awesome," I told her. "I'll get right on it!"

At lunch, Alivia, Kacy, Danielle, and Emily weren't sitting at our usual square table. Today they all sat at a long rectangular table with Logan, Mateo, and a bunch of other boys from the basketball team. Perfect. It would be just the right time to put my Danielle and Connor plan into action.

I unwrapped my sandwich, ham and cheese rolled in a tortilla, and took a bite, chewing as I listened to Alivia tell everyone that she sold over three hundred cookies and brownies today and was thinking of adding blondies to her menu.

"Those are our favorite, right, Logan?" Alivia said, smirking.

"I like Reese's Peanut Butter Cups," he started to say, when Alivia elbowed him. "Oh," he said. "Right. Blondies."

I swallowed and looked down the long table at Alivia and Danielle. "You guys have so many more pastries today," I said. "You must have been baking all weekend. Will they last all week, or do you have to do more?"

Last week, they had been running out every day.

Danielle twirled a strand of brown hair around her finger. "That's the great thing about working with a partner. Alivia decided it would be faster if she did all the baking herself, so now I just have to do the other stuff."

"I had a few glitches starting out, but now that I've figured out the secret, I'm sure I'll have plenty of treats," Alivia said, smiling.

I looked at Alivia and couldn't help feeling impressed. "I hope you don't have to spend all your free time baking," I said. "It takes me forever to collage my Claragrams. I barely have time to do homework anymore."

Alivia waved her hand like she was brushing my words away. "It's no big deal. I'm a fast worker."

I was about to say something else, like, she had to have more than one oven, when Eli stood up and shouted, "Mateo's in love with the lunch lady!"

All of the boys at the far end of the table laughed.

"Shut up," Mateo said, staring at his lunch.

"No, it's the principal," Ryan screamed. "He's dreaming of Dr. Bingley."

All the boys laughed again.

Danielle leaned forward and whispered to me and Emily. "I think he's too embarrassed to say who he really likes."

Emily nodded. Her fair cheeks flushed a pretty shade of pink, and her eyes flashed over to the tables by the door of the cafeteria where Joey and his friends usually sat. Emily blushed more than anyone I knew. Just thinking about being embarrassed made Emily feel embarrassed.

I glanced back over at Mateo. His usual goofy self seemed to shrink and disappear as the boys named even more and more unlikely crushes. I knew how terrible it felt to have a group of people ganging up on you. Even if Mateo's friends were more friendly than mean-spirited.

"Hey, you guys," I said. "I learned this really fun game."

Everyone at the table stopped talking and looked at me. Mateo took a deep breath and finally straightened up.

Alivia scooted closer to Logan and stole one of his potato chips.

I'd been thinking about using this game in my match-making business for a while but hadn't found the perfect couple for it yet. Danielle and Connor were just right.

"First I need two volunteers. Danielle and Connor, would you help me?" I asked before anyone else could even think about volunteering.

They both stood up next to our table, and I pulled two long pieces of colored yarn out of my backpack. Thankfully the art teacher had been willing to help me out this morning. Each piece of yarn was tied in a loop at either end. I hooked the strands of yarn around each other, then put the two ends of the blue yarn around Connor's wrists and the two ends of the orange yarn around Danielle's wrists.

"Okay, you guys, here's your challenge. You have to unhook from each other, but you can't take the loops off your hands and you can't cut or destroy the yarn. And you have to stay attached to each other until you figure it out. Or until lunch is over."

"That looks so easy," Logan said.

I smiled. "That's what makes it hard."

Danielle and Connor were standing about a foot apart next to our table. Danielle was giggling, but she looked happy. Connor was smiling at her. "I've got an idea," he told her. "I'll hold my arms out and you step over my yarn, okay?"

Connor held his arms as wide and low as possible, and Danielle stepped over his yarn so they were standing even closer. But they were still tangled. The only difference was that now Connor practically had his arms around Danielle.

"I think you need to go under the yarn," Logan called out.

Danielle reversed her steps and climbed back over Connor's yarn and then went under it. They were still tangled, but now they were both laughing. I didn't think they cared if they solved the puzzle.

"I'm going to the lobby," I said, standing up. "I need to get the store ready for lunch hours. But I have one more set of strings. Kacy and Ryan, want to play?"

"I got this!" Kacy said, grabbing the strings and slipping the loops onto her and Ryan's hands.

"Want help?" Emily asked me, not looking up from the game on her phone. "I already refilled the Kisses and questionnaires after I passed out the Claragrams."

"That's okay," I told Emily. "You stay and hang with everyone." Business hadn't been busy at all today, so there wasn't that much to do. But maybe now with two new happy couples in the works, things could go back to normal.

Chapter Fifteen

It was impossible to go to my locker in between every class. I usually went first thing in the morning, before and after lunch, and once more in the middle of the afternoon right before social studies. But on my way to the Cupid Clara table, I realized I left my red folder in my backpack, so I had to detour to get it. When I arrived at my locker, it was covered in mini Reese's Peanut Butter Cups. Someone—all right, not someone, my secret admirer—had taped the little gold foil cups all over the front of my locker so they spelled out:

HI, CLARA.

U R SWEET.

I looked up and down the hallway to see if anyone was around, but I was the only one there. I tried to pull off one of the candies, but it was really stuck on good. If I took the time to clear off my locker I'd be late to the Cupid Clara table. I had no choice. I'd just have to leave it up until the end of the school day and hope not too many people noticed.

When I got back to the lobby, it was already filling up with people. Alivia and Danielle were unpacking more boxes of cookies, and Logan was talking to them as usual.

"I'm so perfect," he said in a high-pitched voice. "I know a perfect game that's really impossible, but I'm going to pretend it's real."

I realized he was making fun of me the same moment Danielle saw me and said, "Hi, Clara!"

Alivia pressed her lips together like she was trying to stop a smile, and my stomach turned into an icy pit. Why was Logan making fun of me? Did everyone in the group want to make fun of me?

"Hey, guys," I said, trying to act casual. I swallowed hard and stepped behind my table, getting set up. As I was checking the questionnaire box to see if any new ones had been turned in, Emily walked up still playing her game and sat in the seat next to me. I sat down and whispered in her ear. "The secret admirer struck again."

She finally looked up from her screen. "Tell me," she said.

I told her about the Reese's cups on my locker.

"So cute!" she said.

"Who's cute?" Mateo asked, walking up to our table. "Me?"

I laughed and handed him a questionnaire. "Didn't you say you were going to fill one of these out for me?"

"Yes, ma'am!" He grabbed the paper and a pen and started filling out the form.

Emily got her phone out and started playing Hoppy Frog again, and a group of sixth-grade boys walked past our table.

"Hey, guys, if you fill out a questionnaire, you'll get some chocolate and the name of a girl who might want to dance with you at the Hot Chocolate Social."

The boys all looked at one another as if they weren't sure.

"You should do it," Mateo told them. He held up his paper. "I'm filling one out."

The boys didn't look completely convinced, but they all took a paper anyway.

I pulled out my marketing/advertising plan and read through it trying to see if there were any other things I could do to help fix my slump.

<pre>
        CUPID CLARA MARKETING/ADVERTISING PLAN
1. Create awareness: People will find out about
Cupid Clara by seeing the store and seeing the
Claragrams, and through, hopefully, word of
mouth.
2. Success stories: Satisfied customers will
encourage other people to give Cupid Clara a try.
3. Flyers? I could put them in people's
lockers.
4. Specials and promotions? Half price?
</pre>

Hmmm. Maybe it was time to give flyers a try.

"Hey, Clara," Mateo said, chewing on the end of his pencil. "What if the girl I like isn't in here?" He tapped our striped box.

"If you already like someone, I'm not sure my questionnaire will help you," I told him. "But you might be surprised by your results. Maybe the perfect girl is out there and you didn't even know it."

"But if I did know my perfect girl, you could still help me." Mateo gave me a huge smile. "Right?"

I laughed. "Sure. I guess."

I sat down next to Emily while Mateo filled out my questionnaire and Emily played her game. Then I said, "I'm worried no one trusts my matchmaking anymore. That's why they're not filling out questionnaires."

"I don't think you even need the questionnaires," Emily said. "Matches are springing up all around you. Without you even trying."

"What do you mean?"

Emily paused her game, then leaned in, cupping her hand around her mouth. "Mateo totally likes you!"

"What? No way!" I scratched my head. "Why would you say that?"

"Didn't he just say he already knew who he liked? And he wants you to help him?" Emily raised an eyebrow.

"That could mean anything!" Emily meant well, but she just didn't have the matchmaking knack the way I did.

"What about the snow day? You told me he showed up at your house with a dish for Sofia's mom? That sounds fishy to me. It sounds like the kind of story you'd make up if you wanted an excuse to see the girl you liked."

I opened my mouth to say something, then closed it again. Emily did have a point. Now I didn't know *what* to think. It didn't feel like Mateo liked me when we were together, but maybe I hadn't been paying close enough attention.

"Here you go!" Mateo announced, handing me his questionnaire. "But I'm not sure that's going to help you match me. I really think we need to have that talk."

Emily kicked me under the table, but I ignored her.

"Sure," I said. "You know where I live. Literally."

Mateo nodded. Then he shoved his hands in his pockets, like he had something else to say but couldn't figure out how to say it. He looked around at all the people gathered at my table and Alivia's table. Then his face brightened.

"I have an announcement, everyone!"

Most people looked at Mateo expectantly.

"Everyone meet on Clara's front lawn for a snowball fight this Saturday at ten a.m."

"What?" I felt a flash of panic, and I tugged Mateo's sleeve. "You can't just invite everyone over to my house. I have to have permission from my dad first."

"I didn't invite them to your house." He grinned at me. "I invited them to your front yard. So get permission."

Emily kicked my foot under the table again. "He wants to hang out with you," she sing-songed out of the corner of her mouth.

"See you around, Clara," Mateo said, winking. Then he leaned in close. "Will you meet me after basketball practice today?"

I nodded, my eyes wide. As he walked away, I glanced at Mateo's questionnaire. Sure enough, his favorite dessert was Reese's Peanut Butter Cups.

Was Emily right? Could *Mateo* be my secret admirer?

Chapter Sixteen

I sat on the floor of the hallway sketching my flyer. On the bottom of the page, I drew a picture of a mug filled with hot chocolate and marshmallows with squiggly lines of steam floating from the top. The front of the mug was decorated with a heart with an arrow through it. Then, across the top of the flyer, I wrote:

**THE HOT CHOCOLATE SOCIAL IS IN
TWO WEEKS!
DO YOU KNOW WHO YOUR DANCE
PARTNER IS?
CUPID CLARA DOES!**

STOP BY THE CUPID CLARA TABLE IN THE LOBBY TO FIND OUT WHO YOUR *PERFECT* MATCH IS!

I made the lettering on the word *perfect* curlicue and fancy, and then put down my pen and looked over my work.

"Hey, Clara. What are *you* doing here?" Alivia's voice interrupted my train of thought. But before I could even answer, she pelted me with another question. "What's that?" she asked, sitting down next to me.

"A flyer for Cupid Clara," I told her. Then I figured I might as well take advantage of getting to hang out with her alone.

"Alivia . . . are you angry at me?" I asked, feeling nervous. "I'm sorry about Logan. I didn't realize he was the guy you liked."

"Oh, he wasn't the guy I was talking about." Alivia's cheeks turned pink, and I got the feeling she might not be telling the truth. "I just decided I liked him this weekend." Then Alivia studied my face. "You're not mad at me, are you? For taking Logan from you? It kind of seemed like you liked him."

Did the whole world think I liked Logan? I shook my head. "I only liked him as a friend. Promise."

Alivia looked at me like she didn't believe me.

"I was trying to fix him up with Emily," I went on. "And now I'm trying to figure out how to get my business back on track." I pointed at my paper. "I thought maybe a flyer would help."

Alivia pursed her lips and looked at me thoughtfully. Then she leaned in and lowered her voice. "I wasn't sure if I should tell you," she said. Then she stopped and looked up and down the hallway. "I'm not saying this is true. It's just what I've heard."

"What?" I asked, leaning in closer as well.

"Well, some people are wondering why they should trust you and Emily to make them a match when neither of you are going out with anyone. I mean, if you guys were *really* good matchmakers, wouldn't you have made your *own* matches?" Alivia raised an eyebrow and shrugged one shoulder, like she was apologizing.

"But I don't have a guy because I don't want a guy," I explained. I could have gone out with Logan. But I decided not to mention *that* to Alivia. Not when she already seemed to think I liked him.

Alivia nodded solemnly. Then she said, "I'm just telling you what I heard. *Some* people, I'm not saying who, think you put those candies on your locker yourself. Just so people would think you had a guy."

My jaw dropped. How could anyone think that? "No way!" I told her. "Can you keep a secret?"

Alivia's eyes widened, and she made an X across her heart. "Totally," she said.

I lowered my voice to a whisper. "I think I have a secret admirer. And I think it might be Mateo. He asked me to meet him after practice."

Alivia looked at the locker room then back at me. She nodded in thought. "I mean, I personally always thought you could get a guy. But the thing is, with Emily it's different. A lot of people think that you can't get anyone to like her."

"That's not true!" I shook my head at Alivia. "We've been focusing on making matches for our business, that's all. Who's been saying all this stuff?"

Alivia looked off down the hallway and squinted her

eyes. "I know this seems harsh, but maybe you shouldn't have Emily sitting at the table all the time. You want your customers to be thinking about happy couples, you know?"

Alivia's words made my stomach feel like a huge, heavy lump of clay, weighing me down. I was trying to think of some way to respond when we started hearing noises from the locker room. The boys were about to come out.

Alivia stood up. I gathered all my things and stood next to her. "You and Mateo and me and Logan should go to the movies sometime," she said.

"I'm not—" I started to explain that I wasn't actually going out with Mateo, but Alivia interrupted me and said, "If you want, I could start telling people I think you're an awesome Cupid."

"Really? That would be great!"

Just then, I heard a loud voice saying, "She probably started this whole matchmaking thing just to find her own guy, but now that I'm taken, she can't get anyone."

It was Logan. He was the first person to come around the cinder-block wall of the locker room. He stopped short when he saw me standing there and blinked at me a few times. Then he looked at the ground.

"Clara!" Mateo bounded happily over to me when he came around the wall.

"Hey," I said, watching Alivia watch me.

"Have fun, you guys," she said, wiggling her fingers at us. Then she linked her arm through Logan's, and they walked off down the hall together. The other players all headed out the door into the parking lot.

Soon Mateo and I were standing alone in the hallway. My stomach began to churn. It reminded me of when I had stomach flu last year, except that my heart was also starting to pound a million beats a minute and my forehead was starting to sweat.

"Thanks for coming," Mateo said. "I've been wanting to ask you this for a while, but it's really uncomfortable. I just didn't know how to do it."

A huge pressure began to squeeze my chest. I felt like I couldn't get a breath. *Was Mateo going to ask me to go out with him?* What should I say?

I didn't think I liked him, but maybe I did. Maybe that's why my body felt like it was about to explode. I'd never really liked anyone before, so how was I supposed to even know what it felt like?

Mateo was nicer than Logan anyway, and Alivia said it would be good for my business.

I probably did like him. That had to be what all these feelings meant. I took a deep breath.

"Yes," I said.

"Yes, what?" he asked, wrinkling his brows in confusion.

A nervous giggle bubbled up from my pinched throat. *Oh yeah.* I should probably wait for him to ask me before I answered. "I meant, yes, go ahead and ask me your question," I explained. "It's okay."

Mateo took a deep breath. "It's about when we were in elementary school together." He put his hand on his forehead and looked down at my feet.

An uncomfortable tingle began to work its way down my spine. "What about it?" I asked, my voice shaky.

He bit his bottom lip and wouldn't look up at me. "If a boy hadn't been so nice to a girl, I mean, he was never mean to her, but he just hadn't been that nice, and now he felt really bad about it. Do you think she could ever forgive him?"

Suddenly all my breath came out in a rush. I hadn't even realized I'd been holding it. Mateo was actually apologizing for being part of the crowd. For not standing up to the bullies. Could I forgive him? I looked at his face. He still wasn't looking right at me, but I could see his eyes, and that let me know that was his feelings were true. He did feel really bad about how he'd acted.

"Yeah," I said softly. "I think she could."

Mateo lifted his head to me in a smile that radiated happiness like sunshine. It was sweet. "So how do you think he should apologize?"

Wow. I was impressed. He wanted to make the apology all official and everything. "He should write the girl a letter. That might make the apology feel more real."

It seemed impossible, but I thought Mateo's smile grew even bigger. "Thanks, Clara, you're the best."

"No problem," I said.

"One more thing," he added, his face turning bright red. "Since I think you know who I'm talking about. Could the girl ever, maybe, like the boy as more than a friend?"

My heart got all fluttery for a second. Could she? I meant, could I? Maybe I was already starting to. "Yeah," I said. "I think she could."

That night, while I was making *tortas* for Papi and me to have for dinner, I couldn't stop imagining what it would be like to go out with Mateo. I tried to picture myself eating lunch next to Mateo, going to the movies with Mateo, and dancing with him at the Hot Chocolate Social. Everything I pictured made my heart to do a little flip. My insides felt like melted chocolate, soft and gooey.

Going out with Mateo would probably also help me stay in the popular group. Would we hang out with Alivia and Logan all the time? I didn't think Logan was that nice, but maybe Alivia would start liking someone else soon. Anyway, Alivia seemed to like the idea of me dating Mateo. So that was good.

"Clara, yoo-hoo. Are you there?"

I turned around and saw my father standing next to me. And the table wasn't even set!

"Sorry, Papi!" I said. "I must have lost track of time."

"It's okay. I'll set the table." Papi grabbed two plates from the cabinet. "What were you thinking about?"

There was no way I was telling Papi about Mateo! "Nothing," I told him.

Papi paused. "I know I'm an old man, but I want you to be able to talk to me. I feel as though lately all you give me is silence and 'it's okay, it's okay.'"

I took our sandwiches to the table and put one on each plate. "You're not an old man," I reminded him. "You're younger than every other dad I know."

Papi filled our water glasses. "But I'm still not cool enough for you to talk to me."

"Papi," I pleaded. How could I explain that I didn't want to give him any grief? "Everything is okay. *Really*."

Papi pulled his cell phone from his back pocket. He started dialing a number. "If everything is okay, then why haven't you called Mami? You won't talk to me, but you have to talk to her." He handed me the phone. It was already ringing.

Tears sprung up behind my eyes. "No," I pleaded.

"We can eat when you are done," he said, walking into the other room.

"David?" I heard my mother's voice squeaking in the kitchen. "Hello?"

I sighed and held the phone up to my ear. "It's Clara," I said, swallowing back the lump in my throat.

"Clara!" she said. I could hear the smile in her voice. "I'm so glad to finally hear from you. It's been a little while."

"Yeah, sorry. I've got a lot going on at my new school this semester." I sank down into my chair at the kitchen table and pushed my plate away to make room for my elbows.

"So your father tells me. Honey, listen, sometimes it's hard for a girl to talk to her father. Especially one who is your age."

"It's not hard to talk to Papi," I told her. "There's just nothing to talk about."

"There's *always* something to talk about," she said laughing. "And the older you get, the more things there will be. Maybe it hasn't started yet, but soon you're going to have a crush. Not to mention all the problems that can happen with girlfriends. You're going to need your *mami*."

"I don't have a crush," I started to say, but stopped when I pictured Mateo's sparkling smile. I felt my cheeks heating up and hoped my mother couldn't tell the truth through the phone.

"I know you aren't used to talking to me yet. We haven't had as much time to grow close as you and your father have had over the past couple of years. And I think when a girl is little it's good for her to have such a strong relationship with her *papi*. But now you need women. If you come to live with me, you'll have not only me but your *abuela* and all your *tías*. Just think about it, okay? That's all I ask."

"Okay," I said. Not because I really was going to think about it, but because I wanted to get off the phone.

"Thank you, baby. Will you put Papi back on?"

I went into my father's office and silently handed Papi the phone. Then I went back to the kitchen to finish setting the table. I loved my mom, I really did, but I was insulted she thought I needed her more than I needed Papi, especially after ignoring us for an entire year. I was sure I wanted to stay with Papi. Somehow I had to show him that I wasn't any trouble.

Chapter Seventeen

Walking into school the next day, I couldn't believe how many people called out my name and said hello to me as I passed. It was weird. Most people had been friendly to me before, but this was more than that.

"I'm signing up for Cupid Clara today," Mari, a girl from my gym class, shouted when she saw me coming.

"Awesome." I smiled, handing her a flyer, even though she'd already decided to be my customer. "Maybe you could give that to one of your friends?"

She tucked it in her backpack. "Sure! And congratulations on you and Mateo," she said.

"Uh, me and Mateo?" I asked. What was she talking about?

"Oh," she said, nodding knowingly. "Got it. Anyway, I hope you can find me a guy as cute as he is."

"Definitely," I said, though I didn't know what she meant, exactly.

When I arrived at the Cupid Clara table, a small crowd was waiting for me, even though it was early. Alivia was unloading the day's pastries. Emily was nowhere to be seen.

Alivia stepped over to me and whispered in my ear. "I told Emily you wanted her to wait by your locker this morning. You're welcome!"

Alivia went back to her booth, and I felt a little pang in my heart as I thought of Emily sitting alone by my locker. But there were people with money wanting to get their matches, and I couldn't leave my table now or even take a break to text her. Not when business had finally picked up again. I'd explain to Emily later.

When the bell rang, I rushed to my locker to find her, but she wasn't there, so I hurried to science and took my seat next to her.

"Hey!" I said. "Sorry about this morning. Business is back. There were so many people signing up!"

"Oh. No problem," Emily said, but she didn't look at me.

She was busy playing that game on her phone again. Actually, about half the kids in our class were playing it.

"Two hundred and thirty-five lily pads!" one kid called out.

"What?" said Emily. "No way. I've never gotten higher than eighty-seven."

"You cheat!" said another kid.

"There's no way to cheat," Emily answered.

Just then, Mrs. Fox walked in. "Phones away. I don't care if the bell hasn't rung yet. The second you walk through my door this is a No Phone Zone." She pointed to the sign on her wall that had a picture of a cell phone in a red circle with a diagonal line across it.

Everyone groaned as they put their phones away, and the bell rang. Mrs. Fox pulled a stack of papers from her tote bag and walked around to the front of her desk. "I have your tests here, and most of you did very well. Good work."

Mrs. Fox began to hand the papers back to everyone, and I felt my shoulders relax. I'd been spending so much time making matches and Claragrams, I hadn't really studied that much. I was glad to hear we'd done well.

Mrs. Fox put my paper on my desk face down, and I flipped it over to see what I got. It took me a second to register that 23/50 was not a good grade. That was only 46 percent. At the bottom of the paper, Mrs. Fox had written, *Please come see me after school*, in green pen.

I flipped my paper back over quickly, looking over my shoulders to see if anyone had seen my results, but if they had, I couldn't tell. My eyes felt heavy and fuzzy, and my chest felt like someone was closing a door on me. I'd never gotten a grade that low in my entire life.

What would Papi say? I had a sinking feeling I already knew. I shoved my test to the bottom of my backpack and paid extra close attention for the rest of the class.

After school, I went to talk to Mrs. Fox.

She told me I'd have to get Papi's signature on my test. I felt tears welling up in my eyes, but I blinked them back. Somehow there had to be a way to convince Papi that this wasn't a big deal. That one test didn't mean I couldn't handle school. I trudged through the snow to my house, trying to decide if I should tell him before or after dinner. When I got to my front door, though, I stopped in my tracks. Hanging from the wreath hook was a big orange construction-paper heart with my name written in brown cursive letters. It sort of reminded me of a heart-shaped Reese's Peanut Butter Cup.

I slowly reached out and lifted the brown ribbon loop off the hook and flipped the paper heart over. A note was pasted in the center of the heart, and my own heart was pounding. Was this Mateo's apology?

I took a deep breath and read it slowly.

> YOU'RE SMART AND YOU'RE FUNNY.
> THOSE THINGS ARE BOTH TRUE,
> BUT YOU'RE ALSO UNIQUE.
> I WISH THAT YOU KNEW.
>
> THE WAY THAT YOU ARE
> IS PERFECTLY COOL.
> YOU DON'T NEED TO PROVE
> A THING TO OUR SCHOOL.
>
> AS YOU PASS OUT YOUR HEARTS
> MAKING MATCH AFTER MATCH,
> I WANT YOU TO KNOW,
> I THINK *YOU'RE* THE REAL CATCH.

When I finished reading, I flipped the heart over and over to see if Mateo had signed the poem. But there was nothing. It was a nice letter, but it wasn't exactly an apology. Did he think that it was? I turned to look at the street.

I don't know why, it's not like I expected to see him standing there waiting for me. But there he was, standing on Sofia's driveway. I waved to him, and he looked both ways before jogging across the street to me.

"Hi," I said.

"Hey." He gave me a funny lopsided grin. "I guess you know why I'm here."

I nodded. "Yep." I held out the heart to him and smiled. "*Someone* left this on my door."

Mateo took the heart, flipped it over, and read the back. Then he looked up at me and laughed. "Someone who thinks you're pretty great," he said.

I grinned. "Someone with really good taste, right?"

Mateo looked right into my eyes and grinned back. My stomach got all fluttery, and my breath caught. Mateo was fun to hang around with, and he'd really changed since elementary school. Plus I'd never noticed how his eyes were such a deep, rich blue. And I liked the way they were always a little crinkled on the edges. Mateo was happy all the time.

Behind Mateo, Joey's front door opened. Joey stepped outside and headed right toward my front walkway. I started to wave, but when he saw me standing there with

Mateo, he changed directions and jogged to his mailbox, like that's where he'd originally meant to be going.

"Hey," I called out to him as he opened the mailbox door and checked inside. He didn't answer, but the box must have been empty because he turned around and headed back to his house empty-handed. I watched him the whole time, but he kept his gaze off in the opposite direction, like he was avoiding my eyes.

"Joey!" I said, as he went up his walkway.

"Sorry," he said, pointing at his sweatshirt. "I'm freezing." He went inside and I turned back to Mateo, my shoulders feeling sunken and heavy.

Suddenly Mateo's eyes went wide like he had just remembered something. "Did you ever ask your dad about the snowball fight? Can we all still come over tomorrow?"

"Oops! I forgot," I said. I didn't add that once Papi heard about my test he wasn't likely to say yes either.

"Well, ask him tonight, okay, because Ryan and Connor planned to ask Kacy and Danielle to go out tomorrow."

"I'll try," I said, even though the thought of asking Papi made my stomach flip.

"Oh, I almost forgot, Alivia told me to tell you she can't wait! And I can't wait either."

Alivia was excited to come to my house? There was no way I was going to let tomorrow's snowball fight get canceled. "Don't worry. I'm sure he'll say yes," I said. "Tell everyone I'll see them at ten."

I went inside and up to my bedroom. I took out my science test and stared at the blue line Mrs. Fox had drawn for my father's signature. If I showed Papi this test, he'd freak out. But I'd work hard and raise my grade, and he'd never have to know. I found a pen in my desk and wrote *David Martinez* in a messy scrawl on the blue line. I knew it was wrong to fake his signature, but it would be more wrong for me to miss my snowball fight and have to go live with my mom for one stupid mistake.

I shoved the test back into my science folder and went downstairs to warm up the *carnitas* Papi had prepared last night. *Carnitas* were my father's favorite dinner. I'd ask him about the snowball fight when he was full and happy.

Chapter Eighteen

It took me forever to figure out what I was going to wear to the snowball fight. Snow pants would keep my legs warm and dry, but they would also make them look puffy. My big snow boots were the only thing that would stop my toes from getting frostbite, but they made me walk like Frankenstein. And then there was the question of my hat. Going to a snowball fight without a hat was begging for someone to dump a bucket of snow on your head. Going to a snowball fight with a hat was risking looking like a dork.

I decided to risk it.

I bundled myself up like I was visiting Antarctica. I even

zipped my coat all the way up to my chin. Then I went out front at ten minutes to ten to set up a card table with a big insulated jug of my special hot chocolate and cups.

"Is that the winter version of a lemonade stand?" Joey called, tromping down his front steps.

I laughed. "No, I'm having some friends over for a snowball fight." A strange flutter beat in my chest for a second as I remembered the snowball he threw at me a couple of weeks ago. I wondered if I should invite him to join us. A part of me wanted to until I remembered how awkward it would be. He wasn't in our friend group. He wasn't even in our grade. It would be weird for him to hang out with us, even if he was my next-door neighbor.

"I'd invite you, but then we'd have an odd number of people. For teams," I stammered, feeling like an idiot.

"Don't worry," Joey said, backing away from me. "I'm only outside to wait for Evan's dad to pick me up. He's taking us to a triple feature of the Lord of the Rings in Chicago."

"Oh," I said, a strange tug-of-war between relief and disappointment twisted my stomach. "I wasn't worried. I mean, it would have been fine if you stayed."

"Right. Just until your friends show up." He looked at me curiously then, like he wanted to ask me another question, but wasn't sure what it was.

"We could have a snowball fight a different da—" I started to say, but at that moment, a blue minivan pulled into my driveway and Logan, Connor, Eli, and Ryan spilled out. Logan instantly grabbed a handful of snow and lobbed it at me. It mostly hit my right elbow.

"Hey," I said, brushing the snow from my arm as the minivan pulled away. "Don't we have to wait until everyone's here?"

Another minivan, this one belonged to Emily's mom, pulled up in front of my house. Emily, Alivia, Kacy, and Danielle climbed out. None of the other girls except Emily were wearing hats. Alivia's hair was hung in big, soft curls. It looked really pretty, like she'd had it specially done.

I pulled my hat off my head and shoved it in my pocket.

"Does anyone know where Mateo is?" I asked. Everyone shrugged. Then Kacy said, "Wait. There he is." She pointed across the street.

"Who's he with?" Alivia asked, wrinkling her nose at the girl in the green ski suit.

I froze. He was with Sofia. What was going on?

"Hey, you guys," Mateo said after the two of them crossed the street. "This is Sofia. She used to go to school with me and Clara. She lives right across the street, so I thought it would be nice to ask her to join us."

"Great!" I said, pretending like I really felt it.

Sofia looked at the ground. "Thanks," she said.

Alivia gave me funny look. I shrugged.

"I was thinking we'd split up into teams of two," Mateo said, and then started explaining how each pair would build their own fort and stockpile of snowballs.

But I couldn't focus on the rest of his rules because Sofia was standing in my driveway with all my friends from my new school. *Sofia!* Not to mention the fact that Joey had been watching the whole thing and now he was slowly backing his way up onto his own porch. My eyes flicked back and forth between Joey and Sofia but finally stuck on Sofia.

"Okay," Alivia announced. "I'll be with Logan." Logan went to stand next to Alivia. She flipped her hair back over her shoulder.

"I call Danielle," Connor said. Danielle smiled and gave me a thumbs-up.

"Kacy, think fast." Ryan tossed a snowball in Kacy's direction. She caught it. "Want to be a team with me?"

"Sure," Kacy smiled. Ryan was the tallest boy in our grade.

I looked around our group. Emily, and Sofia, and I still didn't have partners, but Mateo and Eli were the only boys left. Everyone seemed to notice what I'd just noticed at the same time. Suddenly there was a lot of awkward shifting. Alivia leaned over to Logan and whispered something. Then she said, "Eli, you should be partners with Sofia. Don't you think so, Logan?"

"Oh yeah. Definitely," Logan agreed.

Eli looked at Sofia like he wasn't so sure. "You ever been in a snowball fight before?" he asked.

Sofia looked at the ground. "I don't need a partner," she said. "I'd be happy to sit on the steps and watch. I'm not really a—"

"I'll be partners with Sofia," Mateo said. My heart twisted a little bit. Why would he want to be partners with Sofia? Was he trying to be nice to her for my sake? Because we used to be friends? I'd rather just have him be my partner.

"That's silly," Alivia said. "Eli totally wants to be her partner. You be partners with Clara. Emily can sit out."

Emily and I both looked at each other. I could see the red splotches working their way over the top of her puffy blue collar.

"Oh, um, yeah," she said to me, taking a step backward. "I don't mind sitting out."

I didn't want to make Emily sit out, but I wanted to be partners with Mateo. I pictured us huddled close together behind our fort, both of us out of breath from the fight. It was too romantic to pass up. I looked at Alivia, unsure of what to do.

"There's no other solution," Alivia pointed out. "It wouldn't be fair to make Emily be a team by herself, and it wouldn't be fair if one of the teams had three people."

Alivia was right. That did make sense. And Emily would understand why I had to be the one partnered with Mateo. After all, she's the one who figured out he liked me in the first place!

"You can be in the next snowball fight," I told Emily.

"Okay. Yeah." Emily took another step backward, not really watching where she was going. It was like she just wanted to get as far away from the situation as possible. She took another step back, tripping over the edge of the driveway and plopping down, bottom first, in the snow. Behind me, I could hear everyone burst into laughter. I sprang forward to give Emily a hand up. When I reached her, I could see the tears shining in her eyes. Then I saw Joey, walking up behind her.

"Hey," he said. "Could I be your partner? At least until I have to leave?"

I looked at Joey, swallowing the urge to shout, "NO!" It didn't make any sense. I should be happy that Emily had a partner.

Emily turned to him, her shiny eyes crinkling in a smile. "Sure," she said. "Thanks!"

Everyone agreed to this plan, and we all got started building our forts along the outside edges of my yard. The center of the yard would be no-man's-land. The forts were really just short walls of snow we could huddle behind with our snowballs. And I couldn't really tell if there was a way to win the snowball fight. Mateo's rules were a little hard to understand.

I got to work scooping and patting snow into a semicircular wall, but most of my attention was on Joey and Emily. Their wall kept falling down, but they didn't seem to mind.

They were cracking up. When my wall was about a foot high, I suddenly realized I was the only one on my team working on it. Mateo was staring across the front yard at Sofia and Eli.

"Hello?" I said, nudging him in the ribs. "I thought we were a team."

"Sorry." Mateo shook his head and looked down at me.

"Our fort's done!" Ryan called out.

"You're all going down!" Kacy shouted.

"No way," Connor yelled. "Attack!"

Seconds later, snowballs pelted down on us, and Mateo and I had nowhere to hide since our wall crumbled instantly.

"Where are our snowballs?" I asked him, looking around frantically. "We have to defend ourselves."

"I forgot to make them," he said, laughing. "I think we just have to wing it." Mateo grabbed an armful of snow, then rushed out into the center of the yard. He threw all the snow in the air, which did nothing except get himself covered in snow. All the other teams were making and throwing snowballs as fast as they could. I quickly ran behind a nearby oak tree so I'd have some protection and started making and throwing snowballs while Mateo stayed in the middle of the yard drawing almost all the snowball fire. It wasn't much help offensively, but at least it meant I wasn't getting hit by snowballs anymore. So much for my plan of Mateo and me snuggling together behind our fort!

After what felt like forever but probably wasn't actually that long, Evan Cho's car pulled up onto the street in front of Joey's house.

"Hot chocolate break!" Mateo announced, and everyone except for Joey and Emily rushed the hot chocolate table.

Joey said something I couldn't hear that made Emily laugh. Then they actually shook hands, and Joey headed to Evan's car. I watched his shoulders as he went, hoping he'd turn around so I could thank him and say good-bye, but he hopped in the backseat and drove off without looking back. Emily headed over to the hot chocolate stand with a secret half smile flitting on and off her face, and a little pang of something hit my chest.

"I'm freezing," Alivia announced. "Can we go inside and watch a movie or something?"

"Uh, sure," I said. "No problem."

"Clara makes the best popcorn!" Mateo told everyone.

"You've watched a movie at her house before?" Alivia asked, raising an eyebrow at me. I felt a smile tug at the corner of my mouth.

"Uh, yeah," Mateo said, looking at Sofia. "On the snow day."

"I call that everyone sits with their partners for the movie!" Alivia said. "Sorry, Em. You don't mind do you?"

Emily's face was as splotchy as I'd ever seen it, but she just shrugged and looked at the ground. "Why would I mind?"

I squeezed her hand and mouthed the word *thanks*. Then I imagined all the awesome matchmaking possibilities of a movie: Mateo's arm around my shoulder, Mateo holding my hand. I took a deep breath and decided to be my own Cupid. "You guys can have the sofa and the floor pillows. Mateo and I call the loveseat."

Chapter Nineteen

Emily didn't show up to the Cupid Clara booth on Monday morning. I hoped she wasn't sick. She hadn't texted me or anything.

Since there was no one else to watch the shop, I closed up the Cupid Clara booth early. I had to go hand my signed test to Mrs. Fox, and I wanted to do it before anyone else was there. Now that I actually had to give it to a teacher, I could see that signing the test myself was one of the worst ideas I'd ever had. But I couldn't erase the signature and ask my dad to sign it for real. The only thing to do at this point was turn it in and hope Mrs. Fox couldn't tell it was fake.

"Clara," Mrs. Fox said when I walked through her door, "I was just thinking about you."

"Oh, um, okay," I stammered.

"I was going to call your father and recommend a tutor for you. Some of the concepts we study this year are quite complex, and a bit of extra explanation can sometimes make all the difference."

"No!" Mrs. Fox couldn't call my dad. Then they'd both realize I'd faked the signature.

Mrs. Fox blinked at me in surprise. "I'm sorry?"

"I mean, a tutor sounds great, but my dad is really busy, he'd never be able to drive me. He doesn't get home until late."

Mrs. Fox pursed her lips and studied me for a minute. It felt like she was probing my brain, and I was sure she'd give me a detention or send me to the principal or something. But instead she said, "There's a student in my eighth-grade science class who might be able to help you out one day a week after school. I'll speak to him this afternoon. Can you come back at the end of the day?"

I nodded, relief flooding my body. "That would be great," I said. "Thank you."

When the first bell rang, and everyone started showing up for class, Emily walked in, healthy as can be.

"Hey," I said. "Where were you this morning?"

"I went to a Mathletes meeting," she said. "Joey suggested I give it a try."

"Oh," I said. "When did he—"

"At your house. On Saturday." Emily pulled her science book out of her backpack, opened it to a random page, and started reading.

"Is everything okay?" I asked her.

"Mmm-hmm," she said, but she didn't look at me. So I got out my book and started reading too.

When I returned to Mrs. Fox's classroom at the end of the day, I was surprised to see Joey standing in front of Mrs. Fox's desk, and Mrs. Fox nowhere to be seen. I felt a flush rise along my collarbone.

"Hi," I said, pausing in the doorway. If I went all the way inside, Joey would realize that I was the student who failed the science test. Maybe I could pretend I was there for another reason. I didn't want him to know I needed extra help. "Do you know where Mrs. Fox is?" I asked pointing at Mrs. Fox's empty chair. "I needed to ask her something."

"Staff meeting." Joey tapped his pencil on the science book sitting on Mrs. Fox's desk.

"What are you doing here?" I asked, still pretending.

"Tutoring," he said.

"I didn't know you were a tutor." I should leave. The longer I stayed, the more chance there was that Joey would realize I was the one who needed help, but I didn't want to go. "That was nice of you on Saturday," I told him. "Being Emily's partner I mean."

"Well, somebody had to be nice to her." Joey's voice was short and curt. I cringed a bit. "It didn't seem like you were going to do it."

I stepped back. It felt like Joey had just spit at me or something. He'd been annoyed with me before, and he'd teased me before, but I'd never heard him so disappointed in me. My whole body felt flooded with shame. I hung my head and mumbled, "You don't understand. It's complicated." As the words left my mouth, I realized how silly they sounded. Of course to Joey it wasn't complicated at all. He didn't care what other people thought of him. "She wasn't even that upset. You're making a big deal out of nothing."

"She acts like she doesn't care, but deep down she does. It might seem like a small, no-big-deal thing to you, but how many no-big-deal things happen to her all the time?" he said. "She deserves better. And I thought you were better. I never figured you for a mean girl."

I swallowed hard to get the lump out of my throat. He was right. I took a step backward. I could see Joey didn't want to talk to me or have anything to do with me. "I'll talk to Mrs. Fox later," I said.

"Wait."

I stopped.

"I'm supposed to tutor you."

Oh boy.

There didn't seem to be any way out of it, then. I set my backpack at a desk in the front row and pulled out my science notebook. For the next forty-five minutes, Joey explained Punnett squares and alleles and Mendel's pea experiments with so much enthusiasm they actually seemed interesting. When Mrs. Fox came back to the room, I was surprised. It didn't seem like that much time had passed.

"I had a feeling this would be a great pairing," Mrs. Fox said, smiling at us. I looked down at the ground. We weren't a pair. It didn't even feel like we were friends right now.

"I'd like you both to come back every Monday afternoon. Would that be okay? I can call your parents if you need me to."

"It'll be fine!" I said quickly.

"I can come," Joey added.

"Great. I'll see you both then." Mrs. Fox sat down at her computer and started working on something, so Joey and I both packed up our bags. We walked out of the classroom, down the hallway, and to the front door before I realized we'd have to walk home together too.

Joey didn't say anything for the first block and neither did I. I didn't know what to say. There seemed to be both a million things I *should* say and also nothing that felt right.

Finally Joey spoke first. "Are you going out with Mateo?" he asked.

I stopped walking for a second and looked at him, surprised. "No. Why do you ask?"

He hiked his backpack higher up on his shoulder and said, "I just heard a rumor, I guess. Plus you seem to be hanging out with him a lot lately."

We walked in silence past the next house. "He's really nice," I told Joey. "I know you probably don't think so, but he's been sending me all these secret letters and they just show that he's not . . . he's not like Logan, okay?"

Joey shot me a frown. "His secret letters prove that?"

Sheesh. Now what did I do? "I can't show them to you. They're private. You'll just have to trust me."

Joey shook his head and gave me another disappointed look. "Your middle name is clueless," he said sadly. "Clara Clueless Martinez."

My mouth hung open, but I couldn't think of a reply. He'd been right about Logan, but he was wrong about Mateo. Mateo was a good guy. I could tell.

Joey left me standing on the sidewalk as he went into his house. A breeze gusted up the driveway, and I shivered, wrapping my arms tightly across my chest. I jogged to my front door and the warmth of my house. As lonely as I used to feel at my old school, I never felt as hollow as I did watching Joey walk away.

Inside, I started working on my Cupid Clara update paper. I probably should have been working on it with

Emily, but I was a little afraid to call her. What if she was even madder than Joey?

Then my phone buzzed with a text. I grabbed it out of my bag, hoping it was from Emily. Maybe she'd let me apologize. But it wasn't. It was a text from an email address I'd never seen before: reesesboy@email.com. It didn't take a genius to figure out who it was, though.

don't take off your winter hat! I like the REAL you.

I read Mateo's words again, and my eyes got slick and shiny. I knew Joey was right. I hadn't been nice to Emily at the snowball fight. Mateo liked the pretend me. That was probably the only Clara anyone would ever like.

Chapter Twenty

The next morning, Emily didn't come to the Cupid Clara table again. This time, though, she texted me.

going to mathletes.

That was all it said.

Working solo was tricky because I couldn't man the table and pass out the Claragrams at the same time. Besides, I really missed Emily. I decided to be extra nice to her at lunch today. Maybe I'd even get back to work on finding her a boy. Maybe that was what was really going on. She'd been the only one at my house on Saturday who didn't have a guy she liked. Maybe Eli would be a good match for her.

When I arrived at our table in the center of the cafeteria,

Alivia was sitting next to Logan, Danielle was sitting next to Connor, and Kacy was sitting next to Ryan. Mateo and Eli sat on the end, so I sat across from them. Emily wasn't there yet. I made sure to leave enough room on the bench for her.

Alivia was talking about the Hot Chocolate Social. During morning announcements, the principal had said tickets would go on sale tomorrow.

"I had the best idea, you guys," Alivia told us. "We should totally do it the way they do dances in high school."

I had no idea what Alivia meant. How could high school dancing be different than middle school dancing?

"I love that idea," Danielle gushed. "But, like, what does that mean?" I was relieved that I wasn't the only one who didn't get it.

Alivia spread her hands on the table. "Okay, so first we'll all come over to my house to take pictures, then we'll all go out to eat, then we'll go to the dance."

"So fun!" Kacy said.

"I guess," Ryan agreed. "But I don't want to go to some fancy restaurant. I want to go somewhere with good food."

Alivia rolled her eyes, but said, "Fine, we can pick the restaurant later. That's not the main thing. The main thing is, I think we should have dates. Like the boys should ask the girls to go to the dance with them."

My eyes darted over to Mateo. I couldn't help it. I felt my heart race a little. If he asked me to go to the dance with him, would I dance with him all night? Would he kiss me good night? The thought made my stomach swoop in a big wave. I had to put down my sandwich for a moment.

"Does that mean the guy has to pay for everything?" Logan asked. "Dinner and tickets and everything?"

Alivia sighed. "That's not the point."

Everyone kept talking about the details of how having dates for the dance would work, but I stopped paying attention when I realized that Emily still hadn't come to lunch. I looked up at the door, expecting her to walk into the cafeteria any second, when I realized she was already in the caf. She was sitting with Joey and Evan and a couple of other kids from Mathletes.

"You guys, look," I said. "Emily's eating with other people." I pointed across the cafeteria.

I was about to ask if I should go ask her to come back and sit with us when Alivia said, "Good for her."

"I'm so glad she found the right friends," Danielle put in.

"But you guys have all been friends since elementary school, right? Aren't you guys the right friends for her?" I asked.

Kacy shrugged. "People change."

"We're different now. Even though it's sad, it's for the best," Alivia said. "Some people are into socializing and cool stuff, and some people are into math, right?"

I nodded, but I didn't agree. Emily liked socializing and math. She just didn't like being treated like she didn't matter.

"If you'd rather go sit with her," Alivia gestured toward Emily's table, "we'd totally understand."

I felt a little urge to stand up and walk to Emily's table, but I didn't move. I stayed where I was.

>>>———▶

That afternoon, all the seventh graders filed into the gym at the end of the day for the ABC assembly. The teachers gave out certificates for Best Business Plan, Greenest Business, and Most Community Positive Business. Then they announced the top five businesses, the ones that would be competing during the final week to see who would get to attend the Future Entrepreneurs Conference.

I was nervous. Emily and I sat in the bleachers one row behind Alivia, Danielle, and Kacy. I could see that Danielle had her fingers crossed behind her back, but Alivia sat with her chin high in the air like she had no doubt that Sweet Alivia's would be one of the chosen businesses. I didn't feel nearly so confident. Mostly because even though there were only about four inches separating me and Emily in the real world, it felt like four miles. Or even four million miles.

"In no particular order," Mr. Bersand announced, "The top five businesses are: Abby's Animals—a pet toy business. Cupid Clara—a matchmaking business . . ."

We made it!

I turned to Emily, full of excitement, but she gave me a calm smile and said, "Good job, Clara," like we barely even knew each other.

"Hoppy Frog—a game app business. Sweet Alivia's—a bakery."

In front of me, Danielle breathed a huge sigh of relief, but

Alivia's expression didn't change. She wasn't surprised to be top five.

"And finally, Clear Walks—a snow-shoveling business."

Once all the businesses were listed, everyone gave polite applause. The winners were all bouncing around excitedly. I was grinning too, even though I could feel Emily's aloofness.

"Congratulations to all our young entrepreneurs," Mr. Bersand said. "I couldn't have been more impressed with the creative ideas and business savvy you all demonstrated. Now it's time to get to work on your final reflection papers including your financial accounting statements detailing your expenses, gross profits, and net profits. Great work, everyone!"

When the assembly was over we all stood up.

"Congratulations, you guys," Alivia said to me and Emily with a funny smile. "May the best girls win!"

"I'm sure it will be you," I told her.

"Thanks," she said.

"Seriously," I told her. "It's almost inhuman how many cookies and muffins you made over the past couple of weeks. You deserve to win just for effort."

Alivia squinted her eyes and me. Then her smile returned. "This is just *really* important to me," she said. "I want to be a pastry chef someday."

"Well, good luck," I said. "Maybe we'll tie for best business."

"Yeah," Alivia said, though she didn't look too excited about it. "Maybe."

>>>————▶

The next day, the school lobby looked like a giant empty cavern now that all but five of the ABC businesses had closed up shop. All five tables sat together near the entrance to the office, and on the other side of the lobby, a new table had been set up selling tickets to the Hot Chocolate Social. It was fun to see so many students who'd gotten Claragrams buying tickets. I bet the dance floor would be packed during the slow dance this year. I'd made sixty-eight matches total, and would probably make a few more.

Before school started for the day, I opened my folder and looked at my list of Matches. Besides my friends, I had a few that were my favorites. Like the couple that almost had the same name, Alex Levine and Alex Levy. Okay, so one was an Alexander and the other was an Alexa, it was still pretty close. I also liked the couple that both raised chickens in their backyards, Eleanor and Matthew, and the couple that both wanted to star on Broadway, Laura and Jeremy. I smiled.

When students started arriving, I sat alone at the Cupid Clara table, offering out questionnaires to all who passed by. But not many people took them. What a terrible time for a slump to be starting again. Especially since Alivia's "date" idea had really caught on. I'd heard a lot of other people planned to bring dates now.

I couldn't figure out what had happened to make my customers disappear again. With the dance so close, I would have thought business would increase. And I couldn't have already reached all my potential customers. There were more than seven hundred kids at Austen. I looked at the other four tables. They all had plenty of customers, so the problem had to be something specific to Cupid Clara.

"How's my favorite Cupid?" Mateo called, sidling up to our table.

"Things aren't so great." I pointed around the lobby. "No customers."

Mateo wrinkled his forehead. "I thought you weren't accepting any new questionnaires anymore, now that the dance was so close."

"What?" I raised my palms in the air. "Why would you think that? I never said that."

Mateo shrugged. "I don't know. I heard it somewhere. One of the guys told me."

I scratched my head. It didn't make any sense. "Well, tell him he's wrong. I'll be making matches right up until the end."

"Sure," said Mateo, leaning against the corner of my table. "So, does everyone know who they're going to the dance with?" He lowered his voice to a loud whisper for that last part and pointed to the ticket table at the other end of the lobby.

Alivia shot Logan a look.

"What?" he said. "I'm waiting to see if my dad will give me the money. Two dinners plus two tickets is way more than my allowance."

Alivia turned purple, so I said to Mateo, "Who are *you* going to dance with? It's not fair of you to ask everyone but yourself."

Mateo looked at the ground. "I haven't asked her yet. I'm going to do it after school one day this week."

I felt a blush creeping up my neck, but then the bell rang, and we all had to go to class.

Emily came home with me after school so we could work on our final Cupid Clara reflection paper and financial analysis. One block ahead of us, we could see Joey walking home alone. It hurt that he wasn't walking with us. I wondered if Joey would ever want to be friends with me again now that he thought I was a jerk. But maybe I could prove him wrong. Maybe I could be in the popular group *and* be a good friend to Emily.

"Are the kids from Mathletes nice?" I asked her.

"You know them. Or some of them, anyway," Emily said, pointing up ahead. She tilted her head, studying Joey. "They are actually really nice. I never have to plan what I say when I'm with them. I even used to be friends with one of the girls, Lexi, when we were in preschool."

"That's great," I said, but a part of me wished she'd told me that the kids were terrible. That she missed me and wanted to come back into our friend group. It was weird. I'd wanted to become closer with the other girls, but now that I was, I missed Emily. I wanted to come up with some way to convince Alivia that she was wrong about Emily. I wanted to show Emily that I still cared.

"I know we have to work on our paper, but you were supposed to be my first match, and I still haven't found you a guy," I said. "Do you want me to work on that today too?"

Emily looked down at the sidewalk. "That's okay," she said. "But I don't want you to make me a match."

"Really?" I turned to face Emily. "I know it didn't work out so great last time, but don't give up. I can make you a great match. I know I can."

Emily shook her head. "I'm not giving up." She lowered her chin and looked at me shyly. Then she looked up ahead at Joey. "I already like someone. I realized it during the snowball fight. I realized a lot of things that day."

I watched Emily as her eyes followed Joey walking up the driveway and into his house. A little smile lit up her face.

Suddenly my ears felt clogged, and every noise, including the sound of my own voice sounded far away. Did Emily like Joey?

I remembered how angry Joey was at the way I'd treated Emily. Did he like her back?

The dreamy little smile still played at the corners of Emily's lips. I couldn't speak. It felt like I had a Claragram wadded up in the middle of my throat. For the rest of the afternoon, I could barely concentrate as Emily and I made the outline for our paper and started inputting all our financial information into our spreadsheet. My ears were buzzing and my stomach was roiling.

When I pictured Mateo in my head, I *knew*. It didn't matter how much I had in common with him, or how good he was for business, I didn't like him in that way. I couldn't like him in that way. I would never like him in that way because there was no spark. Because he didn't have that indefinable something. Because he didn't make me feel like I wanted to be a better person. Because he wasn't like . . .

The realization hit me like a snowball, smack in the face.

I could never like Mateo because he wasn't Joey.

I liked *Joey*.

And not only would he never be my boyfriend, I wasn't even sure if we were friends anymore.

Chapter Twenty-One

When I said good-bye to Emily that evening, it felt like I was saying good-bye to her forever. Of course, I wasn't. I'd see her at school the next day, but our friendship would never be the same. She'd start going out with Joey and hanging with the Mathletes, and I'd never be able to tell her how I really felt.

As I started preparing dinner for me and Papi, I was pretty sure my life was as bad as it could get, but I was wrong. Papi walked through the front door at 6:45.

"What are you doing home so early?" I asked.

Papi shook his head at me. "I just got your progress report from school today."

My stomach dropped. I'd forgotten that at Austen teachers posted progress reports midway through the marking period.

"Progress reports aren't final grades," I reminded him. "And I'm doing really well in most of my classes. Cupid Clara is one of the top five businesses!"

My fathers' face softened. "I'm proud of you. But you are flunking science."

"I've just been really busy working on my business," I explained, feeling flustered. "And science has always been my hardest subject, but I'm working on it. I even have a tutor!"

"I know," Papi said, giving me another stern look.

I didn't think my stomach could feel any lower, but now it felt like my entire middle had flattened like a tortilla. How did Papi know? Maybe Joey's father had told him?

"I called your teacher," he explained. "She was very confused that I didn't know you were struggling in her class. She told me that was why she asked me to sign your test."

I swallowed hard. This wasn't good.

"But I didn't sign anything."

The water for the rice began to boil over, and I quickly turned it off. My father's expression didn't change. It was like he hadn't even noticed the sizzle of water as it splashed over the edges of the pot and onto the stovetop.

"*Lo siento*," I whispered. I didn't trust my voice to get any louder. I'd probably start crying. Papi didn't get angry very often, but when he did, he got very angry.

"'I'm sorry' is not good enough. You need to explain." He folded his arms across his chest and looked at me expectantly.

I nodded but didn't say anything. I couldn't. I couldn't let Papi see that my whole life was a great big mess.

"Clara, I don't know what to do anymore. You keep telling me that everything is fine, but then I find out it's not fine at all. Your *mami* is right. A girl your age needs more than just a father." He rubbed his hands all over his face and blew an exasperated sound between his lips. Finally he shook his head. "Maybe it would be better for you to live with her."

The tears started slipping silently from my eyes. This couldn't be happening. "Papi, no, *por favor*," I begged.

"We won't make any decisions until this summer." Papi wouldn't look at me. His shoulders were low. "Go to your room and finish your homework. I'll make dinner tonight."

The next few days, I felt like I was a zombie: On the outside, I looked like all the other seventh graders at Austen, but on the inside, my feelings were dead. The only thing I could think about was the fact that it didn't matter what happened at Austen anymore since next year this wouldn't even be my school.

When I went to Mrs. Fox's room at the end of the day to meet Joey for another tutoring session, I could barely get my eyes to focus on the paper in front of me. What was the point? I'd already messed up. It couldn't get any worse than it already was.

After a few minutes, I realized that Joey wasn't explaining anymore. He was staring at Mrs. Fox's lab safety poster. I couldn't believe Joey wasn't going to be my next-door neighbor anymore.

"What's the matter?" he asked. I was surprised to hear how caring his voice sounded. Maybe he didn't totally hate me. Or maybe all our years of friendship meant that even though we weren't friends anymore, he still didn't want me to be sad.

I sighed. I might as well tell him. "I think Papi is going to make me go live with my mother."

Joey put his hand on my shoulder. "Why would you think that?"

"Because I'm too difficult to handle," I told him. "Because I'm a horrible person."

A huge sob bubbled out of my chest before I could stop it. I jumped up, covered my mouth, and ran out of the room. I tore down the hall to the girls' bathroom. I raced into the nearest stall, grabbed a handful of toilet paper, and started wiping myself up when I heard the door open.

"Hi, Marigold, it's Alivia."

I froze. After Joey, Alivia was the last person I wanted to see me with snot hanging out of my nose. I slowly climbed up onto the toilet seat so my legs would be hidden from view, and waited.

"For tomorrow, I want four dozen mini muffins, six dozen cookies—half chocolate chip and half oatmeal M&M—plus five dozen kitchen-sink brownies. Great, we'll be by to pick them up on the way to school, just like always."

I shook my head because I couldn't believe my ears. What was Alivia doing? *Ordering* her baked goods? How could she be turning a profit if she had to be paying someone else to be her baker? And why hadn't she told anyone that was what she was doing?

I pressed my knuckles against my mouth. I was so dumb. Alivia hadn't told anyone because she was cheating. It was the only thing that made sense.

"Bye," Alivia said just as I heard the door swing open again.

"Clara?" Emily's voice echoed off the tiled walls.

"Clara?" Alivia repeated, sounding panicked. There was a shuffling of feet. I thought she might be checking under the stalls. "She's not in here."

"Oh," Emily said. "Sorry. Somebody told me she was upset. I thought she might be in here."

"Wait," Alivia called out. Emily must have been about to leave.

"Yes?" Emily's voiced echoed in quiet bathroom.

"I wanted to explain," Alivia said. "About yesterday."

Yesterday? What was going on? I should probably clear my throat or something. This eavesdropping thing was going too far, but I stayed frozen as a statue. I couldn't help myself.

"You don't have to explain," said Emily, "but you do need to confess to Mr. Bersand. Otherwise I'm going to tell him."

Had Emily found out that Alivia wasn't really making her own products too?

"It was an innocent mistake," Alivia crooned. "I *really* thought that you and Clara weren't accepting any new questionnaires. It was, like, a public service to let people know."

That's why no one was coming to our booth anymore! I couldn't believe it. I knew Alivia could be moody and kind of self-centered, but I thought she was my *friend*.

"Maybe it was a mistake, and maybe it wasn't, but you still need to tell," Emily said firmly.

"And what if I don't? Are you going to tattletale? Because that would be a huge mistake. Look at yourself: You have no fashion sense, you don't even make any effort to be cool, all you care about is schoolwork, and you are a total suck-up to all the teachers. The only reason that everyone doesn't call you out for being the loser that you are is because you *used* to be my friend. Go ahead and tell on me, and then have fun becoming the joke of Austen Middle School."

There was total silence in the bathroom. I could feel it pressing down on me like I was underwater. I imagined Emily staring at Alivia, frozen, terrified of becoming an outcast, just like I had been. And then suddenly, a hot swirling anger began to build inside me, rising through my stomach and my chest, swelling and swelling until I thought I might explode. I planted my feet on the ground and slammed my palm against the bathroom stall door. It burst open and hit the next stall with a loud crack.

Alivia and Emily both jumped, and then stared at me in shock.

"She"—I pointed at Emily and glared at Alivia—"is not a loser."

I took a step closer to Alivia and realized for the first time that I was taller than her. By an inch. I straightened myself up and took another step forward. "Emily is cooler, smarter, and nicer than you will ever be. And she is great at styling hair and doing math. She has *real* talent, not like *some* people who pretend they are good at baking but really just hire someone to do it for them." I put my hands on my hips. "Sound familiar, Alivia?"

All the color drained slowly out of Alivia's face. She could lie about our questionnaires and there would be no way to prove she was sabotaging us on purpose, but she couldn't wriggle her way out of this one.

"I don't know what you're talking about," Alivia said, cocking her head to one side. "But I can see why you guys are friends. You're both so annoying. You make a perfect match."

"I'd rather be annoying than mean and selfish," I said. "And even though I can't win the ABC, I'm glad you can't win it either, because if you don't tell Mr. Bersand, then *I* will. And I don't care if you make me an outcast. Your opinion doesn't matter to me anymore."

Alivia blinked at me, her mouth opening and closing stupidly. I didn't wait for her to come up with a reply. I turned and headed out of the bathroom and back to Mrs. Fox's room. Thankfully Joey wasn't there anymore. I gathered up my things and started to walk home.

I strode out the front door and into a gentle snowfall. I tilted my head back and caught a couple flakes on my tongue. My whole life was ruined, but for some crazy reason, I felt great.

"Clara! Wait up."

I turned around and saw Emily running and sliding through the snow to catch up with me. When she tried to stop, her feet skidded on the ice and she crashed right into me.

"Sorry," she said, steadying herself on my shoulders and standing up straight.

"No. I'm sorry," I told her. "I've been a terrible friend to you. I thought being popular was the only way be free of the old Clara."

"But why would you want to be free of yourself? You are awesome."

"I used to be a loser," I explained, feeling tears threaten again. "My only friend wasn't even a friend. She was just the other person who didn't have any friends. I guess . . ." I looked down at my feet. "I don't really know how to act with a real friend."

Emily shook her head. "You were never a loser. You just went to school with a bunch of idiots who couldn't see how cool you are."

"Thanks," I said. "You don't have to be nice to me after the way I treated you."

"I'm not being nice. I'm telling the truth." Emily shivered. "I'm freezing," she added.

"You should go inside," I told her.

Emily nodded and started walking away. I turned and kicked a clump of snow as I began to walk home.

"Clara!"

I turned around. Emily had her arms wrapped around herself and was hopping from foot to foot. "Since Cupid Clara will be finished soon, why don't you come to Mathletes next week?"

"Mathletes?" I asked, wrinkling my nose.

She laughed. "You'll love it! It starts at seven," she called, running back into school. I wasn't so sure I'd love Mathletes, but it was a huge relief to know that Emily didn't hate me anymore. And whatever else happened, at least I still had one friend. A real friend. Just the thought made my shoulders feel warm and loose. I took a deep breath and tilted my head back toward the sky. It was cold, but the sun was out, and I could feel its gentle heat against my cheeks.

When I got home, Mateo was waiting on my front steps.

Oh, no. He was probably here to ask me to the Hot Chocolate Social. I took a deep breath. There were so many reasons why I couldn't go to the dance with him now. First, I didn't actually like him. I could see now that I'd never liked him as more than a friend. Second, I wasn't part of that group anymore. I couldn't just show up at Alivia's house for pictures with Mateo on the night of the dance. And I didn't want to! But mostly, I was done with boys, matchmaking, crushes, dances, and anything that had to do with love. Even when I was being totally careful with my heart, it had still caused me all kinds of heartbreak.

"Hi, Mateo," I said, walking up my driveway.

"Hi," he said, standing up. "I was almost about to leave. Why are you home so late?"

"I had to stay after school," I explained. "But before you say anything, I have to tell you something."

Mateo looked surprised, but he said, "Sure."

"Okay." I took deep breath. "Please don't be mad, okay? I really like you and think you are a great guy, but I like you as a friend."

Mateo nodded. "I like you as a friend too."

"I mean, I only like you as a friend. Nothing more. I can't go to the Hot Chocolate Social with you." I tried to make my expression as friendly as possible. "I'm really sorry, but I'm sure there are tons of girls who will want to dance with you."

Mateo wrinkled his eyebrows and gave me a confused expression. "Did you want to go to the dance? I can't go to the dance with you."

"Yeah," I said, nodding. "That's right."

"No," Mateo shook his head. "*I* can't go to the dance with *you*."

Why was this so confusing? "That's what I said. I know you came over here to ask me to the dance, but I'm saying no."

Mateo got a really sad expression on his face. "I'm so sorry," he said. "I thought you understood. I didn't come over here to ask you to the dance. I came over to tell you I asked Sofia. She said yes! And it's all because of you and all your matchmaking help."

"Wait, what?" I asked in surprised. "You asked Sofia? You like *Sofia*?"

"Yeah," he said. "I told you, remember? The girl who used to get teased?"

I threw my hands up in the air. "I thought you were talking about me!"

Mateo blinked a couple of times. "Oh yeah," he said. "I guess I forgot people used to make fun of you. Sorry."

I looked at Mateo. I was so obsessed with my own tortured past that it didn't even occur to me that people wouldn't remember it. I felt a pang of regret for wasting so much energy on trying to hide the old me, but I also felt a new sense of relief.

"I have to go," I told him. "And that's great about you and Sofia. I'm happy for you."

I went to open the door, when I noticed an envelope taped to the doorknob with my name in a heart on the front.

"From you?" I asked Mateo.

He shook his head. "Nope. See you around."

I opened the envelope and found a ticket to the Hot Chocolate Social, a package of Reese's Peanut Butter Cups, and a note.

NO MATTER WHAT IT SEEMS LIKE, MY FEELINGS FOR YOU HAVEN'T CHANGED, SO I KNOW THE HOT CHOCOLATE SOCIAL WON'T BE THE SAME WITHOUT YOU. MEET ME BY THE AUSTEN ARCHER AT 7 P.M. ON THE NIGHT OF THE DANCE. THERE IS SOMETHING I'VE BEEN WAITING A LONG TIME TO ASK YOU.

I looked at Mateo walking away up my street. If it wasn't from him, who could it be from? I didn't even want to try to guess.

I couldn't believe I used to think I knew so much about making couples. Maybe I could match strangers sometimes, but when it came to my own life, I didn't know anything. I'd spent so many years hiding my feelings, that maybe I didn't know or understand my own feelings at all anymore. Or anyone's feelings. I thought Alivia was my friend, but she wasn't. I thought Logan liked Emily, but he liked me. I thought Emily wasn't good enough, but she was the best. I thought Mateo liked me, but he liked Sofia. And I thought I liked Mateo, but I liked Joey.

And if I was so wrong, so stupid, about so many things, who knew what else I had all wrong? I thought Papi would send me away if he knew the truth of how complicated things were for me. But he already wanted to send me away, so maybe I needed to tell the truth anyway.

Chapter Twenty-Two

All the next day, I tried to plan how I would talk to Papi. Sometimes I thought I should call him at work. Sometimes I thought I should write him a note. In the end, I decided I would tell him at dinner. That was where we had most of our best conversations.

"Clara!" a familiar voice called out when I walked through the front door after school. A woman's voice.

My heart began to race. Was Papi sending me away already? Was I too late to have my conversation? I ran into the kitchen and saw my mother stirring two mugs of hot chocolate.

"What are you doing here?" I asked, sinking down at the kitchen table.

"I talked to Papi yesterday and took the first flight out this morning. It sounded like you needed someone to talk to." She came over to give me a hug, and her perfume smelled like I remembered.

"You flew out here just to talk to me?" I asked doubtfully, too surprised to hug her back. "Are you going to make me go home and live with you?"

"No, baby. Living with me is your decision. I really want you to, but more than that, I want you to know that you can talk to me. I haven't been the world's best mother, I know, but I'm going to do better now. I want to do better."

I swallowed hard, but my heartbeat slowed. Maybe it wouldn't be so bad to talk to her a little bit. Maybe that was one of the other things I had been wrong about.

We took our drinks to the couch, and I told her what it was like for me at Holy Cross after she left. She cried a lot, but she didn't interrupt or apologize or explain. She just listened, which was exactly what I wanted. Then I told her everything that had happened this year at Austen, every single way that I had been totally wrong and silly. She didn't have much advice, but just telling someone made me feel better.

"*¡Dios mío!*" my mother said when I was done, both of us sniffling. "You have a knack for drama. But you have a very good heart, Clara. It's time you start listening to it and trusting it, you know?"

"I think so," I said.

She smiled at me slyly. "So," she said, "little Joey Fano?"

"He's not that little," I said, laughing. "He's taller than Papi."

"Taller than Papi!" My mother laughed, too. Then she got up and beckoned me into the kitchen, where she began to open cabinets and peer through the refrigerator. "I think we should make *carnitas*, and maybe *tres leches* too?"

"Sounds good," I said, my stomach growling.

My mother and I spent the afternoon talking and cooking, and when Papi got home at seven thirty, she and I were both sitting at the dining room table waiting for him. His face fell when he saw both of us sitting there together.

My mother stood up. "Sit down, David. I just remembered a phone call I have to make."

Papi sat down as my mother left the room. At first, we both sat there silently, then I said, "Papi, I don't want to make you sad, but there is something I need to tell you."

My father started to say something, but I stopped him. Then I told my dad the whole story, from the way the kids at Holy Cross treated me, to all my crazy misunderstandings at Austen. When I finished, Papi leaned forward and put his face in his hands.

"I was supposed to take care of you," he said sadly. "I was supposed to protect you from the pain and instead you protected me."

"I didn't want to be too much trouble for you," I told him, feeling choked up. "You always said things would have been better if my mother went to college, which meant everything would be better if I was never born. I didn't want to give you any more reasons to wish me away."

Papi's eyes grew shiny. He looked up at the corner of the ceiling. "I would *never* wish you away. You are the most precious thing in my life, Clara. When I say that it would have been better if your mother went to college, I don't mean it would have been better for *me*. I mean that for a young person, it's better to know your own heart before you decide to share it with another. Your mother didn't know what she wanted when we got married, and I was too young and too in love to realize that I couldn't be everything for her. But she gave me you, and I could never be sorry for that."

Papi leaned forward and gave me a kiss on my forehead.

"I don't want to live with my mother," I told him. "I want to stay here with you."

"I want you here too, but, *mija*, you can't hide things from me. You have to trust *me* to protect *you*."

I nodded my head.

"Do you forgive me?" he asked. "For not protecting you better before?"

I gave Papi a big hug. "I don't need to forgive you," I told him. "You didn't do anything wrong."

Papi held me at arm's length. He looked thoughtful for a moment, then he said, "It was very wrong of you to fake my signature, but now I understand. Still, it better not happen again."

"It won't." I held one hand in the air. "I promise."

My mother knocked softly against the doorframe. "Is it okay if I come back now?"

Papi looked at me and I nodded, wiping my eyes with the back of my finger.

"She's an amazing girl," my mother told Papi as she pulled the pork out of the oven and began to shred it. "Thank you."

Papi and I got up and helped my mother bring the food to the table. When we all sat down again, I said, "I want to keep living with Papi."

My mother nodded. "I understand."

"But maybe I can come stay with you for two months this summer," I suggested, feeling hopeful. "And maybe we can start talking on the phone more than once a week." Even though I was still a little mad at her for everything she'd done, I knew she was sorry, and I knew I needed to learn to forgive.

Now my mother's eyes got shiny. "I'd love that," she said. Then she laughed. "It will be better than a telenovela!" My mother turned to Papi. "So much drama, this one."

>>>———————

My mother gave me a ride to school the next morning on her way back to the airport.

"Papi told me your matchmaking business made the top five," she said as we pulled up to the front of my school. "Congratulations. I'm so proud of you. Maybe you will start your own dating company someday?"

I shook my head. "It was fun," I told her, "but match-making really isn't for me. I liked making the Claragrams, though. I might try joining art club this spring."

"Yes!" my mother said. "Try everything you like. That's the way to find out what you will love."

I gave my mother a hug good-bye, then waved at her as I walked into school. This morning was the final ABC assembly where they would announce the winning business. The entire school got to attend.

Emily and I sat together in the front row.

"Who do you think will win?" Emily asked me anxiously. "Everyone's business is so good. I don't have any idea."

"Me neither," I said, biting my lip.

Mr. Bersand stood at the podium and asked everyone to be quiet. He made a little speech about all the wonderful goods and services everyone bought this year, then he told us we'd raised over $9,000 for charity. Everyone clapped.

Finally he held up a gold envelope with the invitation to the Future Entrepreneurs Conference.

"This year's most successful business is . . ."

He paused and Emily double-crossed her fingers on both hands.

"Hoppy Frog!"

Emily screamed and began clapping so loudly her palms had to be stinging. "That was such a fun game!" she told me while all around us people cheered. "If we couldn't win, I'm glad it was them. Yi Ling's in Mathletes," she added, nodding toward the beaming winner.

Mr. Bersand continued. "Their addictive game was a hit not only with Austen students and faculty, but also made the top one hundred games in an online app store last week."

"Woo!" Emily shouted again.

"Thank you to everyone for helping us through another successful year of the Austen Business Challenge. You may now return to first period."

Emily and I stood up.

"Are you upset?" she asked me.

"Not really," I said, surprised to realize I didn't feel too overwhelmingly disappointed. Even if Alivia hadn't spread those rumors about not taking more questionnaires, I don't think we could have beaten Hoppy Frog. "I think everything worked out the way it was supposed to."

"Hey, are you going to the Hot Chocolate Social tomorrow?" Emily asked. Then she lowered her voice and leaned in close to me. "I think I'm going to do something crazy."

"What?" I asked, starting to feel a little nervous as we walked out of the gym.

"I'm going to ask a boy to dance!" Emily giggled. "Can you believe it? Me?"

"Who?" I said, my voice coming out squeaky. "Joey?" I didn't say more. Despite my feelings for Joey, I wanted Emily to be happy.

Emily looked at me like I was crazy. "Why would I ask Joey? I'm going to ask Evan." She gave me a funny little smile. "I never really stopped liking him, you know."

Right. *Evan.* Of course. A pang of guilt stabbed my chest as I remembered insisting Logan was the perfect guy for her. "I have a feeling he never stopped liking you either."

"I hope so." Emily's eyes sparkled. "Joey told me Evan talks about me all the time." Emily blushed as she and I walked slowly down the hallway toward science. It felt nice to be hanging out with her again.

"Did you hear about Logan and Alivia?" she asked me.

I shook my head. "No, what?"

"They broke up. Eli asked Alivia to go the Hot Chocolate Social, and she said yes. Apparently Logan only asked her to go the dance, but not out to dinner."

Emily and I walked into our classroom and sat in our seats. A part of me felt bad for Logan. He wasn't the nicest guy, but that didn't mean I wanted bad stuff to happen to him.

"You never told me," Emily said as the bell rang.

"Told you what?" I whispered.

"If you're going to the Hot Chocolate Social."

Mrs. Fox pulled out a box with slides, gloves, and little tubes of liquid. "Okay, everyone, today you are going to bleed for science. We are going to find out our blood types. Please arrange yourselves in partners or groups of three."

Emily and I didn't even have to discuss it: We were going to be partners. I went right back to our old conversation. "I'm going," I told her. "To meet my secret admirer."

She raised one eyebrow at me, and I told her about the ticket on my front door.

"Oh no," she said, putting a hand over her mouth. "What if I was right all along? What if, after Alivia said no, Logan decided to give you the ticket he bought for her? What if *he* never stopped liking *you*?"

I shrugged. I doubted that. "I've pretty much learned that whenever I think I know who likes who, I'm wrong. Whoever it is, I will meet them and tell them I'm not interested. Nicely, of course."

"Of course," Emily said. "But isn't there *anyone* you like?"

I felt all my blood rushing to my cheeks. There wasn't going to be any left in my fingers to do the blood-typing test. I looked down at my desk. It didn't matter if I liked anyone. I had no chance with Joey anymore. I shook my head, but Emily didn't buy it.

"I knew it," she squealed. "You don't have to say who."

"Please send one person from your group to the front of the room to pick up your lab supplies," Mrs. Fox announced. I stood, walked to the supply table, and grabbed a box marked *Group #6*.

"Do you want to come over to my house to get ready

together?" Emily asked when I got back. "I could do your hair, if you wanted."

I nodded. "That sounds like fun."

"And if your mystery guy doesn't turn out to be your dream guy, maybe you could do what I'm doing and just ask him yourself."

My heart skipped a beat at the thought of asking Joey to dance. It hurt so much to think about him saying no. Even after all the couples I successfully fixed up, the thought of trying to make my own match was terrifying. It would be much safer to forget the whole thing. Then I remembered my mother's advice. If I didn't try what I like, I might not find what I love.

Could I really be brave enough to ask Joey to dance?

Chapter Twenty-Three

Emily styled her hair in a crown of braids that made her look like a movie star. She gave me a twisted, low side pony-tail. It draped softly over my shoulder. We both wore a little bit of mascara and peach-colored lip gloss. My dress was green with a poufy skirt, and Emily said the color brought out my eyes. Emily's dress was a pale pink and she looked beautiful. I hadn't realized how fun it would be to get all dressed up.

When Emily's dad dropped us off at the front of the school, I reached out and squeezed her hand for just a second. There was no one else I'd rather be arriving at the dance with.

We went inside, and the lobby was totally empty. No traces of the ABC or the ticket table anywhere. We could hear the music thumping from the cafeteria. Most of the songs were going to be fast dances, and I planned to dance with Emily the whole night. But first I had to go to the Austen Archer.

"Wish me luck," I told her, my stomach tightening.

"It's going to be fine." Emily giggled. "Keep me posted, okay? Good luck!"

Emily headed toward the cafeteria, where the dance would be, but I didn't go with her. I waved and headed off in the opposite direction. The Austen Archer mural was over by the gym, and I had a seven o'clock appointment.

My heart began to beat faster the closer I got, but I already knew what I was going to say. No matter who it was. I would say I liked him as a friend, but I didn't want to go out with someone unless it felt right in my heart.

I turned the corner and saw a boy. He was facing the mural, so his back was to me. He wore black dress pants and a pale green button-down shirt. He definitely looked familiar, but I couldn't figure out who it was. Maybe that tall, gangly boy in my gym class? I'd forgotten his name.

"Hello?" I said.

When the boy turned around, I gasped. It wasn't the boy from gym class.

It was Joey.

He smiled shyly at me.

"What are you . . ." I blinked. "I'm supposed to meet . . ." My heart thudded. "But what are you doing here?" I blurted.

Joey's smile faltered. He took a step toward me. "I thought you would have figured that out by now," he said. "I'm the person who's been sending you those notes."

My chest was squeezing and expanding, squeezing and expanding, like an accordion. "*You?* But I thought you didn't like me anymore. Because I was such a bad friend to Emily?"

"Clara." Joey reached out and grabbed my hand, just for a second. Then he dropped it and wiped his palms on the legs of his pants. "I really like you. I've liked you all year. I was bummed to see you acting like a mean girl, but I never thought that was the real you. I'm crazy about the real you." His cheeks colored. "But if you don't feel the same way, just tell me. I'll never mention it again and we can go back to being friends."

I shook my head. I couldn't believe what I was hearing.

I reached out and grabbed *his* hand for a second, then dropped it. "I do feel the same way," I blurted, feeling the blush in my face. "I think I always have. I do want to be friends again . . . and I also want to be more than friends." My heart pounded. I couldn't believe I had just said that out loud!

Joey smiled at me, his chocolate-brown eyes sparkling behind his lopsided glasses. He reached for my hand again, and this time he didn't let go. His skin felt warm and dry against my palm. He leaned forward a little bit, and a waft of his coconut shampoo made my heart flip and then stop.

I wasn't just holding my breath, I was holding everything about me, my breath, my heartbeat, my thoughts, even the cells of my body. Joey leaned a little closer, his exhale warming my cheek. I closed my eyes and then felt the softest, sweetest pressure against my lips. He tasted like a Reese's Peanut Butter Cup.

My first kiss!

When he pulled away, I opened my eyes, and my whole body raced back to life, like I was a video game arcade where the power had just come back on after an outage.

Everything was whizzing and buzzing and bleeping and flashing. And Joey was still holding my hand.

Joey and I walked into the cafeteria. The ceiling was covered with glittery snowflakes, and a sideways disco ball made it look like snow was falling down the walls. Joey squeezed my hand and I squeezed back. I decided hand holding was my new favorite thing.

"Okay, everyone," the DJ announced. "It's that time, find yourself a partner 'cause we're going to slooooow things down a bit."

Joey started pulling me toward the dance floor, but I hesitated because I wanted to tell Emily what had happened. When I searched the room for her, I saw that she was already on the dance floor, dancing with Evan Cho. When I caught her eye, she smiled and gave me two thumbs up.

Joey and I joined them on the dance floor, and when he put his hands around my waist, shivers zinged up and down my spine. I wrapped my arms around his neck and let him sway me back and forth. The music was soft and romantic, the kind of music that might have made me roll my eyes before. But not now. Joey spun me around, and I closed my eyes and let my head rest for a second against his shoulder. For the rest of the slow dance, it felt like we were the only two people in the world.

When the music ended, Joey and I headed over to the refreshment table.

"I have something for you," he said, reaching into his pocket and pulling out a heart-shaped Reese's Peanut Butter Cup.

"So," I said. "Peanut butter and chocolate, huh?" I thought back to the snow day, the day he insisted I'd love peanut butter in my hot chocolate. Even though he was constantly challenging me, I also felt more comfortable around him than anyone else.

He grinned. "What can I say? They're my favorite."

I unwrapped the candy and took a bite. I had to agree.

Peanut butter and chocolate belonged together.

Find more reads you will love . . .

When you're stuck with the name Beauty, people expect beauty and grace and courage from you. And when you're a prince, you're supposed to be athletic and commanding and brave and tall. But when Beauty and Prince Riley's lives turn upside down, Beauty has to figure out just who she wants to be. And Prince Riley has to learn that even a beast's appearance can be deceiving.

The Last Present

A Willow Falls book from the author of *11 Birthdays*

WENDY MASS

SCHOLASTIC

wish

Amanda and Leo know something about birthday magic. When their friend's little sister, Grace, falls into a strange frozen state on her birthday, they'll have to travel in time to fix whatever's wrong. As they journey back to each of Grace's birthdays, they start seeing all sorts of patterns . . . which raise all sorts of questions. Amanda and Leo will have to travel much further than they ever imagined to save Grace.

Sometimes boys, friends, and cooking are the ingredients for drama. . . .

you're bacon me crazy

suzanne nelson

wish

SCHOLASTIC

Tessa loves working at the trendy food truck her aunt runs in their native San Francisco. But her dream turns into a nightmare when popular, arrogant Asher starts working at the truck! He can't make a sandwich to save his life, *and* he's frustratingly cute. But when the city's big food festival is canceled, the future of the truck is suddenly at stake. Can Tessa and Asher set aside their differences and work together?